The Secret of
Ryker's Ford

Ryker's Ford is a peaceful town, with only a few drunks to disturb the easy life of Marshal Warren. But trouble starts when the stage is held up, all the passengers killed and important mail goes missing.

Pinkerton men arrive on the scene but the killings continue, and soon there is a lynching party. A pattern of revenge going back to the days of the Civil War begins to emerge.

A confession and a shooting seem to solve everything but one more act of revenge is necessary. . . .

0121   KINGSTANDING
464 5193   LIBRARY

Loans are up to 28 days. Fines are charged if items are
not returned by the due date. Items can be renewed
at the Library, via the internet or by telephone up to
3 times. Items in demand will not be renewed.

Please use a bookmark

Date for return		
22. JUL 05.	APR 06	'1 3 MAR 2014
AUG 05	- 4 SEP 2010	1 0 JUL 2015
20. AUG 05	2 1 SEP 2010	2 1 JUL 2015
05.	1 4 OCT 2011	1 8 NOV 2016
	1 1 SEP 2012	- 2 FEB 2018
24. SEP 03.	2 2 OCT 2012	2 3 FEB 2018
	2 5 OCT 2012	

Check out our online catalogue to see what's in stock,
or to renew or reserve books.

www.birmingham.gov.uk/libcat

www.birmingham.gov.uk/libraries 2 9 NOV 2022

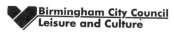

Birmingham City Council
Leisure and Culture

Birmingham
Libraries

The Secret of Ryker's Ford

Tom Benson

A Black Horse Western

ROBERT HALE · LONDON

© Tom Benson 2005
First published in Great Britain 2005

ISBN 0 7090 7739 4

Robert Hale Limited
Clerkenwell House
Clerkenwell Green
London EC1R 0HT

Typeset by
Derek Doyle & Associates, Shaw Heath.
Printed and bound in Great Britain by
Antony Rowe Limited, Wiltshire

ONE

Dusk was falling as the two men rode their tired horses along the trail towards the noisy spate of water that flowed coldly from the distant hills. The birds went silent as the sun vanished and other sounds took over to herald the night and different creatures on the move.

It had been a hot day and cooled rapidly once dusk fell. Men and animals were weary and a hot fire with a meal were what was needed. There was plenty of fuel among the sparse grass. Bits of broken and dried mesquite were soon piled into a heap to make ready the coffee and fry the bacon.

The younger man did most of the work. He was tall and well built, in his twenties and with a dark, broad face and hooked nose. His companion was heavier and some thirty years older. His grey hair was short and neatly trimmed and his features similar to those of the other traveller. They were unmistakably father and son. Their horses were not small cow-ponies, but larger animals, well saddled and carrying brands that would have been strange to any locals who saw them.

The fire soon blazed and the men sat down to eat. They talked softly and watched the moths fluttering round the flames while tiny bright eyes from other creatures blinked curiously from beyond the radiance of the light. The horses drank at the edge of the water and then turned their attention to the lush foliage that grew there. It was all quiet and peaceful as the moon rose in a cloudless sky.

But somebody was watching them.

He lay in the folds of a lichened slope that bore tufts of tall grass. A shotgun was in his hand and his horse was tethered some distance away. He watched the two men finish their meal and clean the tin dishes with dry sand. They laid rifles at their sides as they settled down for the night, and soon seemed to doze off.

The watcher stayed patiently for some time. He wanted to be sure that they were asleep before he made a move. His eyes blinked as insects moved across his line of vision, and he now and then brushed away vinegarroons that crawled over his hands. A lizard came to look at him, its tongue darting out as it threw a long shadow under the newly risen moon.

The man rose silently and moved over the sandy ground with the shotgun cocked and ready for use. He halted some fifteen yards away from his sleeping prey and levelled the weapon. Then he hesitated, his finger trembling on the triggers. He moved a little closer to make sure that the spread of shot would not be too great. Then he levelled the gun again, aiming at the dark mound that was the head of the younger sleeper.

The explosion and the flash broke the rhythm of the night. Birds flew in panic from their roosts, creatures scattered across the ground, and the bitter smell of burnt powder filled the disturbed air. The body that was wrapped in blankets gave a shudder and then lay still.

The older man scrambled to his feet, cursing vividly as he grabbed the weapon at his side to cock and fire at the killer who loomed from the darkness.

His aim was wild and he dropped the single-shot rifle to reach for the pistol at his belt. It was one of the new unwieldly Colt Army models and he cocked it with a shaking hand as the man with the shotgun ran nearer, pulling the trigger on the second barrel as he closed the distance.

The older man stumbled as the charge of shot caught him in the chest. He staggered backwards across the smouldering fire and rolled over amid a cloud of sparks. Then all fell silent again.

Ryker's Ford was hardly a town. It lay as one straggling street along the bank of a tributary of the Gila river. The only reason for its being was that

Amos Ryker had discovered the crossing a few years back and used it to get his cattle down to Mexico or to do a little trading below the border, of which the territory authorities might not approve.

He set up a ferry that earned a few dollars for the owner when the river was too high in the spring and late fall. Then a few stores and a saloon appeared, and over the years, folks settled to profit from the flow of cattle, hogs, and horses. Some came to search for gold, but a little copper was all that seemed to exist in the area.

Now there was a war further north with Confederates and Yankees belabouring each other and needing animals that communities like Ryker's Ford could supply. The little place was having a sudden boom and folks were cheerful despite the fact that most of them sympathized with the South and the war was now looking bad as the Northern armies pushed their way to victory.

Amos Ryker ruled the place as some sort of unofficial mayor. He and the newly arrived banker were the dominant citizens, and it was their efforts that brought outlying ranching folk to the little place where deals could be done and rival armies supplied without anyone getting too involved in a war that seemed a distant comic opera.

Bill Adams and his sons were driving a herd of horses towards Ryker's Ford as dusk began to settle over the hot landscape. There was water ahead at

Mungo Creek where they could spend the night, and then make a final trek the next day that would land them at the ford where they could cross into Mexico.

The horses had originally been meant for the Confederate army over to the east, but Bill Adams was no fool. The Rebs were in retreat, their treasury was near empty and the new issue of paper money could soon become worthless if they lost. He needed cash, and Mexican pesos were better than new Confederate bills or the old issue of Texas dollars that were now almost waste paper. He would have liked Yankee money, but there was no way through to the Northern armies now, and it was too great a distance. His best bet was the Mexicans with their heavy silver coins and no questions about brands. They had a war of their own against some foreign emperor and needed supplies.

The animals smelled the water and quickened their pace. Bill and his two sons exchanged cheerful grins at the prospect of camping for the night and eating a hot meal. The creek hove into sight as the sun vanished over the horizon. The horses headed straight for the sweet water while the men dismounted, unsaddled their own animals and began to light a fire.

It was young Jack who spotted the bodies.

'Pa, come over here!' he shouted as he stood with an armful of dry brushwood and stared down at the pile of bones and torn-apart clothes.

The other son joined him and Bill Adams knelt down to examine what remained of the dead men. Animals and insects had done their work and no flesh was left. The sand partly covered the whitened bones and the clothing had faded in the harsh sun and scouring wind of the hot days.

'Now, ain't that the weirdest thing you ever did see?' Bill Adams murmured as he looked around. 'Get a fire goin' here, lads, and let's see what this is all about.'

His sons hurried to obey and the older man took out a vesta to light a small lamp that he removed from his saddlebag. He watched while Fred and young Jack piled up the dried wood and set it alight. The brightness almost hurt the eyes as Bill Adams started probing among the bones.

'Well, I reckon as how they've been here a coupla weeks or more,' he said quietly. 'There's one helluva lotta buckshot in the back of this fella's skull and I can see some in the ribs of this other fella. The clothes is good store-bought stuff, but there ain't much else to tell us a tale. No guns, no money, and no horses.'

Young Jack knelt at his father's side. He was a thin youth and had never seen dead bodies before. His face was pale in the fireglow.

'How did they get here, Pa?' he asked almost fearfully.

10

'Well, they sure as hell didn't walk, son. They got no boots.'

Fred came to join them. He was less impressed by death and had already put water on to heat for coffee.

'They was bushwhacked,' he said. 'Horses took, and everythin' else worth having.'

'You have the right of it there, lad. Not a lead cent or a scrap of blanket. I figure as how they made camp for the night and then was shot in their sleep. We'd better put what's left under the ground, decent like.'

'Shouldn't we leave it to the folks at Ryker's Ford, Pa?' Fred asked. 'They'll have a preacher and a burial ground.'

Bill shook his head. 'They might have a marshal as well,' he said flatly, 'and we don't want no lawman holdin' us up while he comes out here to look around and then gets back to the ford. We could lose two days or more. We'll just dig a hole, say a few words, and forget the whole thing.'

'Can we have somethin' to eat first?' Jack suggested hopefully.

His father grinned as he stood up and brushed the sand off his pants.

'I reckon so,' he agreed. 'They ain't goin' no place. One thing's for sure though, we take turns at keepin' watch tonight. I'd sure hate to wake up with a charge of buckshot in my ass.'

They slept well enough in the cooler air and

woke just after dawn to start digging out a small trough where the two bodies could be buried. When it was done, the three men stood around with their hats in their hands, and both sons looked at their father for guidance.

'You goin' to say a few words, Pa?' Jack asked.

'I ain't no preacher-fella,' the older man grunted. 'Let's get the hell outa here. And remember, not a word of this at Ryker's Ford.'

They saddled up their mounts a short time later, rounded up the grazing horses, and got ready to leave. It was Jack who spotted something dark among a clump of mesquite. He picked up a battered Stetson, gave it a shake against his leg, and tried it on for size. It was too big and he threw it to his brother in disgust. The other man grabbed it and found that it fitted perfectly. He let out a whoop and all three grinned.

Bill Adams stood thoughtfully for a moment or two, then took the hat off his son's head. He looked at it carefully and checked the leather lining. It bore a name and he read it out aloud.

'J.D. Hudson.'

'Mean anything, Pa?' Jack asked.

'Never heard of the fella, but it gives me an idea. When we get to Ryker's Ford, we'll hand this in to the mayor or the marshal, or whoever's the boss-man. Say we found it on the trail near here. But no mention of bodies. That way there'll be no delay, but if these fellas has kinfolk, they can come out here and look around.'

Jack nodded understandingly.

'We'll be doin' a sorta service, Pa,' he mused.

'That's it, son. Like good Christian folk.'

TWO

Marshal Warren was fast asleep. His feet were tucked under the desk, his large hands were folded across an ample belly, and his snores filled the office. It was a normal condition for the lawman of Ryker's Ford after a good meal and a cup of coffee laced with cheap whiskey.

He had a young deputy, and left most of the work to him. This was based on his often stated principles that the lad needed experience. Marshal Warren was the cousin of the mayor, and the mayor was Steve Ryker, son of the founder of the now prosperous town which had grown since the end of the war nearly twenty years ago.

The war was just history to most folks now. The telegraph had come, there was a weekly stage in both directions, money was stable and the Yankees ruled the roost. There had been a second gold-rush along the banks of the Gila, which had brought great profit to the area. There were now three saloons, two hotels, and plenty of stores which sold goods from the big cities up north and east. Ryker's Ford was a town worth living in: a peaceful, go-ahead place.

The opening of the jailhouse door awoke the marshal. He blinked in the late-afternoon light and took up a pen as he tried to look as though he had been at work on some important matter.

His cousin entered the office, bringing with him an aroma of cigars and Cologne. Mayor Ryker was a small man, thickset and with a hard, sly face that housed piggy eyes, set deeply beneath bushy brows. He was plainly dressed as became a mortician, and his podgy fingers held an unlighted stogie.

'The stage is late, Bert,' he snapped angrily. 'They should have been here before noon, and it'll be dark in a couple of hours. What are you goin' to do about it?'

'What am I goin' to do?' The marshal sat up in his chair. 'I ain't the Wells Fargo clerk, Steve. I ain't gonna do nothing. Maybe they got delayed by somethin' or other. What's Mike Penning doing? It's his bundle of rattlers.'

The mayor leaned over the desk.

'For what it's worth, Bert, you are the marshal of this town. Mike Penning has already telegraphed to the last relay station. They left there at seven this 'mornin' without any problems. They had fresh horses, the mail, and two passengers. So where the hell are they?'

Bert Warren knew when he was defeated. He got up from the creaking chair and went across to the window. He stared out as if looking for inspiration as he scratched his unshaven face.

'I'll send young Abel out to back-trail the stage and see what's happened,' he said as though making some great decision. 'I reckon as how one of the horses has slipped a shoe or something.'

'You'll go with him,' the mayor snapped angrily. 'The whole town is waitin' for the mail, and if they see the marshal sittin' here on his ass, it'll make our family look a right bunch of gophers. Now get out there and earn the money we pay you.'

Before the lawman could make a reply, Mayor Ryker had stormed out and slammed the door behind him.

Bert Warren reluctantly went round to his deputy's lodging, called him out, and then set about saddling horses and loading his guns in case they were needed. The two men rode out about half an hour later.

It was a well-worn trail they were following, and they rode in silence as the mounts picked their way along the ruts. Young Abel was a fair, well-built man with a slightly vacant face that actually belied his quiet intelligence. He was a lad who knew when to keep his mouth closed in a town that gave him a steady job and was run by folks who were all related to one another. He just did his job and watched what happened.

16

Night fell with its usual suddenness and Marshal Warren decided to make camp rather than risk the horses losing their footing in the rough patches of gravel and tufts of dried grass that littered the rutted stage-route.

They set out again in the early dawn, worried now by the non-appearance of the stage. They had only gone two miles or so when they were confronted by the curious sight of bushes blocking the trail ahead of them. They were cut-down lengths of mesquite, freshly hacked from their bases and toppled for some twenty feet or more along the route taken by travellers to Ryker's Ford. The marshal got down from his mount and stared at the barricade.

'And what the hell would that be for?' he mused as he took off his hat and wiped a sweating forehead. 'Ride round it, boy, and see what's goin' on back there.'

Abel Davis did as he was told, steering his horse across the rough ground and travelling some twenty feet or more until he was back on the rough trail. The stage coach was there, and bodies lay on the ground around it.

He shouted to the marshal and got down from his own animal while the lawman came to join him. The horses were still harnessed to the stage, and all four animals looked almost pleased to see human beings for once. They were thirsty and there was little pasture within reach. The driver lay on his face by the left rear wheel. He had been shot through the head. His guard was on the other side of the trail, a shotgun under his body, and several wounds in his chest.

One passenger lay near the open door. He was a large man, dressed in a grey city suit, and at first glance appeared to be unarmed. But just the edge of a derringer poked out from under his right elbow. The gun was cocked and the single barrel still charged. It was the fourth man who merited their inspection. He was also dressed in town clothes, but they were dark and worn. Two Colt .44 pistols lay near him and he wore a belt under the coat, which was packed with cartridges. Both guns had been fired.

'Well, this is sure one hell of a mess,' Bert Warren muttered as he looked inside the rig and examined the luggage of the two dead passengers. One had clearly been a whiskey-drummer. His case of samples lay on the luggage rack. A bullet had pierced it and some of the liquor had leaked on to the leather seat below. The rest of the luggage seemed to be untouched.

'Was there a strongbox on board, Marshal?' young Abel asked quietly.

'They reckon not. Just the mail and two passengers, is all I was told. And these hold-up fellas don't seem to have took nothin' at all. Now, ain't that the strangest thing? Why in hell attack the stage and not take what's on offer? That whiskey-drummer is still wearin' his watch, and them two Colts is worth every cent of fifty dollars. Don't make no sense, nohow.'

Bert Warren started walking round the scene of the hold-up. He was looking at the ground and noting every mark on the sandy gravel. Young Abel watched him, knowing that the lazy and incompetent lawman was at least a good tracker who knew every sign from an unshod mule to a crawling rattler. The marshal eventually came back to stand by the rig.

'Well, as I see it from their horses,' he said thoughtfully, 'there were three of 'em. They blocked the trail to bring the stage to a halt, and then fired from them rocks over there, I reckon. They went for the passengers as they got out the doors furthest from the gang. I also figure that one of the killers is maybe wounded. Either him or his horse. There's some blood back there. Not a lot but it could be enough to need a doctor.'

He looked around in complete puzzlement.

'But why in hell didn't they take the guns and the carpetbags these fellas was carrying? See if there's money in their pockets, lad.'

Abel did as he was told, his hands shaking a little at handling the bodies of the freshly dead men. He found a total of more than twenty dollars in bills and coin, plus two silver vesta-boxes and a silver cigar-case.

The marshal shook his head in bewilderment as

he looked around.

'So where's the mail-bag?' he asked.

They found it under the driver's seat and it appeared to be untouched. The two lawmen set about clearing the trail and piling the bodies into the rig to take to Ryker's Ford. They hitched their own horses to the rear of the stage and were about to climb aboard when the marshal beckoned young Abel to join him near a little pile of burnt material a few yards away.

'Take a look at that lot, young fella,' he said. 'I ain't so good at this kneelin' down business no more, but I'd sure like to know what was burnin' here. Some of it's been blown about but see if you can pick anythin' out.'

The deputy knelt down in the gritty sand and carefully stirred the ashes with his fingers. It had been a pile of papers, some of which crumbled away in a black heap at his touch. There was a tiny white portion here and there and the young man began to pick out what he could from the general mess.

'This here was an envelope, Marshal,' he said as he stood up again, 'and these little bits seem to be written on. Like some fella was sendin' a letter.'

'We'd better take 'em back to town,' the lawman said. 'Just in case them councilmen say we ain't doin' our job properly. Now, let's get the hell outa here.'

*

None of them liked being in the mayor's cramped office. It was at the back of his mortician's business and had a vague smell which some of the councilmen were busy drowning with the whiskey that was freely available. Mayor Ryker sat at his worn desk and the others gathered round him on bentwood chairs which were far less comfortable than his own. The tall, thin figure of the saloon owner dominated. He almost looked like one of the bodies on which the mayor had built such a prosperous business.

Ray Bonny was a gaunt man with sallow face and high cheekbones that sprouted greying whiskers. His eyes were deeply sunk and his mouth was a narrow, ruthless line that seemed set in a permanent sneer. He owned all three saloons in the town and was said to have other business interests which were not defined but which the banker next to him knew about. Banker Stanley was a little bundle of a man, sweating and bald, with a babyish face belied by the hard eyes and professional smile of the moneylender.

The councilmen stared at the marshal and his deputy as they stood like servants, still dusty from their journey. They had duly reported what had been found and now fell silent as the Wells Fargo clerk made his contribution.

'The whiskey-drummer was a fella by the name of Campbell,' he said huskily. 'He comes to town every year at about this time, Mr Mayor.'

Ray Bonny nodded agreement. 'Gets an order from me, he does,' he grunted grudgingly. 'Best whiskey in the territory. We're drinking it now.'

'And the other fella?' the mayor asked.

The clerk looked at the sheet of paper in his hand.

'Don't know nothin' about him, Mr Mayor. Just a man by the name of Fontaine. Nothin' else. He was stoppin' off here and had booked from Tombstone.'

'Doesn't his luggage tell us anything?' the banker asked.

The marshal looked at his deputy and then decided to answer for himself.

'Not a thing. He had money, and a few odds and ends in his pockets. But there's nothin' there to tell us what he did for a living.'

'But why was the stage held up?' the banker asked almost peevishly. 'There was no strongbox and nothin' appears to have been stolen. Can you explain that, Marshal?'

'Damned if I can, but I got me one idea that might be worth throwin' in the tub. There was that pile of burnt paper I told the young fella here to collect and bring back to town. They coulda been letters, so maybe the stage was held up to destroy them.'

He turned to his deputy.

'Show the mayor what we got, lad.'

Abel Davis took the few charred bits of paper

from his pocket and laid them on the desk. All heads craned forward to get a better look and the mayor motioned Abel to bring them round to where he sat. The young man meekly obeyed.

Mayor Ryker picked up one of the little snippets and looked hard at the few words that were written on the blackened fragment. He held it closer to his eyes, and after a silent study, looked at the men in the room with a slight smile on his face.

'It's part of an engraved letter-heading,' he said. 'Some sorta business correspondence.'

He checked through the rest of the pieces, then looked round the office with a contented air of conquest.

'There are several letters here. One is about some bank robbery, another seems to be part of a wanted poster, and this I got in my hand is from the Pinkerton Agency.'

'The detective fellas?' the marshal asked.

'The same. I can just make out part of the heading. And a few words on this little piece. Somethin' about a Mr Hudson.'

'And who the hell is Mr Hudson?' the saloon-keeper asked sourly. 'We ain't got nobody by that name in town.'

The Wells Fargo clerk gave a discreet little cough and they all turned their attention to him.

'I've been sortin' out the mail that was on the stage,' he said apologetically, 'and I reckon as how there's somethin' right peculiar about it. There ain't no mail for the marshal's office. And that ain't never happened before.'

'It sure as hell ain't,' the lawman growled. 'Do you reckon as how all that burnt-up stuff is my official mail?'

The mayor nodded. 'I guess so, Bert,' he said grimly. 'Some fellas didn't want the law to get a particular letter.'

'But who the hell is this Hudson fella?' the marshal whined peevishly. 'I never heard tell of him.'

'I have,' the banker said thoughtfully. 'I recall now that about eighteen or twenty years ago some fellas came into town with a hat they found out on the trail. It had that name in the lining. Nobody ever made claim to it.'

THREE

Ray Bonny stalked back to his main saloon. It was optimistically named as the Lucky Chance. Those who played the gambling-tables there could have testified that all the luck seemed to go to the house. The saloon owner was not a man to give fools a run for their money. He cheated and connived like a Washington politician.

There was a slight grin on his face now. On him it looked more like a sneer in that death's head visage. His right hand was playing with the large gold-nugget that hung from his watch-chain, and there was a certain air of contentment about him. It might almost have been a feeling of relief.

He walked through the double doors and up the stairs with barely a nod to the bartenders who were polishing glasses in an effort to look busy at that time of the day. His own rooms were comfortably furnished and overlooked the back of the large wooden building away from the noise of the main street. He threw open the door and stepped on to the rich Turkey carpet – to be confronted by two men who stood like statues in the middle of the room.

Ray Bonny was taken aback for a moment and reached for the gun under his black coat. Then he realized who they were. His hand relaxed and went back to fondling the gold-nugget that adorned his waistcoat.

'What in hell's name are you doin' here?' he asked angrily. 'I told you never to come to this place. You could upset everything.'

'We're in trouble, boss,' one of the men said humbly. 'Pete's hurt bad and he needs a doctor.'

Ray Bonny cursed as he threw his hat on to a chair and poured himself a drink without offering one to his two visitors. They were tall men, middle-aged but still slim. Their worn clothes looked travel-stained and their hard faces needed a shave. They seemed ill at ease in the fine surroundings of Ray Bonny's comfortable room.

'I hope nobody saw you,' their boss said as he thought things over.

The taller of the two men shook his head.

'We came up the back stairs.'

'So what happened out there?'

'Everythin' went off just as you said. The stage was on time and we killed the driver and guard without any trouble. The whiskey-drummer just held up his hands, but it was the other fella who started it all. He pulled a coupla guns and blazed away like some maniac. He got Pete in the side before we settled with him. We opened the mailbag, burnt all the letters addressed to the marshal, and then rode the hell out so that Pete could get some help. We gotta have a doc look at him, boss. He's hurt real bad.'

Ray Bonny nodded thoughtfully.

'Where is he now?' he asked.

'About a mile outside town. In that old cabin by the stone quarry.'

The saloon-owner made up his mind.

'Right, here's what we'll do. I'll take the doc out there and line his pockets well enough to keep him quiet. He owes me one or two favours, so I reckon on how it bein' collectin' time. You two make yourselves scarce. The law is lookin' for three hold-up fellers right now and I don't want you caught. I look after the people who work for me, and I aim to see us all retire rich and healthy.'

He gave what passed with him as a sympathetic smile while he patted them both on the arm and led them to the door.

'And some good news has come outa all this,' he told them. 'That Pinkerton agent was not after us. He had some other game he was playing. A fella named Hudson who seems to have vanished some time durin' the war. I reckon we're safe as long as we go on operatin' well away from here. So get outa sight, lay low, and wait for me to pay you a visit at the usual place.'

He watched them go down the back stairs, then crossed to the window that overlooked the corral and the rutted lane where their two horses were tethered. The men appeared, mounted the animals, and rode quietly away to the outskirts of Ryker's Ford.

Ray Bonny waited for a while, then went down the same stairs to saddle his own horse and head out in a different direction.

It took only fifteen minutes to reach the old quarry where stone had been hewn years ago to help build Ryker's Ford when the boom times started. The quarry had long since closed down and the few huts were in ruins. Once the little town was constructed, there was no market for the reddish sandstone and no transport suitable to expand the business to other places. It was now a straggly mass of uneven gouges in the rocky hills that housed only a few lizards and an assortment of spiders.

Ray Bonny made straight for the hut where his little gang had occasionally met when he wanted them near the town to receive their orders. The turf roof was partially collapsed and the wooden door lay across the opening, rotting away and covered in sand. The saloon-owner dismounted and called out.

'It's me, Pete. Ray Bonny!'

As he tethered his mount to a broken rail, he heard a weak voice answering from within. The hut was dark and stank of decay. He had to blink a little to accustom his eyes to the place. Pete lay against the far wall. He was a man of about fifty, short and stout, with a haggard face and a beard that was mottled with dirt and spittle. He wore a thick flannel shirt and was pressing his folded waistcoat against his right side. There was not a great deal of blood and Ray Bonny guessed from experience that the bullet was still in the wound.

'How are you feeling, fella?' he asked as he knelt down by the man.

'Pretty bad. Did you bring the doc?'

'No, he was outa town deliverin' a baby,' Ray lied easily. 'But don't worry none, I got all you need right here.'

Pete's eyes took on a more hopeful look.

'We stopped 'em, boss,' he said proudly. 'Eddie got that Pinkerton fella well and truly.'

'So he told me,' Ray said drily, 'but you sure as hell made a mess of the whole thing. It was supposed to look like a hold-up, and you left every-thin' there. That made the folk in town suspi-cious.'

'I was bad hurt,' Pete protested. 'We just stopped long enough to burn every letter addressed to the marshal, just like you said.'

'Yeah, so I heard, and it was all a waste of time. He weren't on to us.'

Pete reached out a bloody hand in supplication.

'Do somethin' about this, boss,' he pleaded. 'I

sure as hell is hurtin' bad.'

'Don't worry, fella. I got just the cure.'

The saloon-keeper drew a short barrelled Colt from under his coat and shot the man through the head.

It took only a few minutes to drag the body from the cabin and dump it in a gully. Ray Bonny was breathing heavily by the time he had finished piling rocks over it and throwing some brushwood on top for good measure. He wiped his hands with a loud slapping noise that startled his horse, and then remounted with a crooked grin on his cadaverous face.

He was too pleased with himself to notice the man who watched from a nearby slope. Every move had been noted and the deputy marshal of Ryker's Ford saw the saloon-keeper ride back to town. Abel Davis had a thoughtful look on his face as he went across to the gully to see who had been killed.

The young lawman was not as stupid as his rather stolid face might suggest. He was only a newcomer in a closely knit community. The marshal was a fat has-been. He left everything to his young assistant and took bribes from everyone who offered them. A deputy had to tread very carefully.

The mayor seemed to be honest enough but Ray Bonny and a few others were lining their pockets at the expense of the local folks. Abel had seen the saloon-owner leave town on quite a few occasions. He would be missing for perhaps a few hours, or sometimes a couple of days. He had no friends or relatives outside Ryker's Ford, and the deputy marshal had become very curious about his absences.

He had also noted that within a week or two of an absence, there would be a hold-up somewhere in the territory. Nothing near Ryker's Ford, and never the stage that came to the little town.

Until now. And that was the strangest hold-up that Abel had ever heard tell of. Everyone killed but nothing stolen. The burned letters were a puzzle. He had never heard of anyone called Hudson, and from what the banker had said, the name went back to when Abel was only a small boy. But something about those letters meant a lot to Ray Bonny back there in the mayor's office. The saloon owner had let a slight smile cross his thin lips. It was almost one of relief, and Abel watched him when he left the others to go back to the Lucky Chance.

His patient observation had been rewarded and he rode back to town feeling very contented.

Mayor Ryker sat grimly at his desk, fingering an unlit cigar and mulling over the tale that Abel Davis had just related. His piggy eyes were half-closed in thought as the young deputy stood nervously waiting for the verdict. It was not long in coming.

'You did a good job, lad,' the mayor said slowly. 'But why did you come to me instead of goin' to the marshal? He's your boss-man.'

Abel twisted his hat between sweating hands.

'I reckoned as you bein' the mayor, and Mr Bonny bein' an important man in Ryker's Ford, it might be better to keep it a little private,' he said, choosing his words with care.

The mayor looked at him shrewdly.

'Yes,' he murmured, 'and the fact that your boss takes a few dollars a week off Ray Bonny might not make him a good listener to your story. You got a head on them shoulders, young fella. Now, as I see it, this dead *hombre* ain't nobody we know, but he seems to be part of a gang of three, and got recently wounded. Could that have happened holdin' up a stage not far from here? Do we agree?'

'I reckon so, Mr Mayor. And the other two called on their boss for help.'

The mayor gave a grim chuckle. 'And Ray Bonny sure helped.' he murmured. 'So what's it all about?'

'I don't rightly know, Mr Mayor, but they was right keen not to let that Pinkerton fella get to town or to have any letters tellin' the marshal about him.'

The mayor nodded. 'So how did friend Bonny hear about the Pinkerton man comin' to town?' he asked. 'The Wells Fargo agent?'

Abel Davis shook his head. 'I reckon not,' he said slowly. 'The agent doesn't get to hear tell of passenger's jobs. Just a name and pick-up points along the route. Somebody either had to ride into town with a message, or it was the telegraph.'

'Old Sid Pearson?' The mayor thought about it for a moment. 'Does he have any connection with Bonny?'

'Always goes in the Lucky Chance after he finishes for the night, and I ain't never seen him pay for a drink.'

'So if a message was sent to the marshal tellin' about this Pinkerton fella, Sid could let Bonny know and the message would never arrive at the jailhouse. You figure that's what happened?'

'Yes, Mr Mayor. I reckon so.'

The First Citizen stood up and came round the desk. He took the young man by the elbow.

'Are you ambitious, lad?' he asked.

Abel Davis did not know the word and the mayor tried again.

'You want to get on in life, son?'

'Sure do, Mr Mayor.'

'Well, that's the right way of thinking. Now, my cousin ain't no shakes as a lawman. He's there 'cos he's my kin, and I've had to put up with it. But he's gettin' on in years and maybe things can happen that will make him think of retirin' and tendin' hogs or suchlike. A smart young fella like you could take over and make somethin' of himself.'

He felt in his waistcoat pocket for a vesta-box to light his cigar.

'Ray Bonny has three saloons and makes one helluva lot of money. He ain't honest folk and my cousin turns a blind eye to the crooked gamblin' and rotgut stuff he sells as whiskey. Now, if it could be proved that Bonny was behind some sorta crime, such as robbin' stages, he'd be due a hanging, if he didn't skedaddle fast.'

'There have been plenty of hold-ups,' Abel Davis said thoughtfully. 'None of them near here and all of them on stages that were carryin' strongboxes. A telegraph man might have that sort of information, Mayor.'

'You and me is thinkin' the same way, son. Now, we gotta wait this out and see what happens. Ray Bonny has no kin, and if he ain't around, there's three saloons goin' up for grabs. Judge Mason and me would have the last word in the matter and it wouldn't do no harm for a young fella like you to have a stake in one of them places, now would it?'

Abel Davis agreed that it would not and the two men parted with the certainty that they understood each other.

FOUR

The stage came through as usual for the next couple of weeks. There were few passengers and young Abel Davis noted their comings and goings. There was nothing of interest to report to the mayor and Ray Bonny never left town or did anything in the least suspicious.

There was one stranger who did interest the young deputy. He was a short, rather scruffy man who rode in on an old mare and put up at Ma Bladon's cheap boarding-house behind the livery stable. The man carried a single gun at his waist, a couple of saddlebags that had seen better days, and looked like some out-of-work cowpoke who had little money to spend.

He was nearer fifty than forty and Ma Bladon welcomed him to her clean little place as the only lodger at a lean time of the year. He told her that his name was Finch and asked her to call him Charlie. She fed him well, noted that he kept himself clean without shaving too often, and neither smoked nor chewed tobacco. He did go for a drink though. And the Lucky Chance was his favourite saloon.

It was in the Lucky Chance that he saw the framed photograph. It occupied pride of place at one end of the bar, clamped firmly on the wall and showing the councilmen posing in their best attire to tell the world that Ryker's Ford had become a town at last. It bore an inked date for ten years ago and had originally been taken by a Tombstone newspaper to record the event.

Below it was a smaller picture, cut out of a newspaper and framed. It displayed the figure of Ray Bonny, standing outside the Lucky Chance where he had recently posed for the Tombstone *Epitaph* during an election for a seat on the territorial legislature. He had not won the seat. There were other ambitious men who had paid the electors bigger bribes.

Charlie Finch examined the photographs with interest and watched the owner of the saloon with shrewd dark eyes whenever Ray Bonny put in an appearance. The saloon-owner had not changed much over the years. He had merely got leaner and more corpselike, but the sneer had never altered and the cold eyes were as dead as ever.

Charlie asked Ma Bladon about him.

'That's one bad fella,' she said with a shake of her grey head. 'Worst thing that ever did happen to this town. I said it when he came here and I say it now.'

'How long ago would that be, Ma?' Charlie asked gently.

'Eighteen or twenty years back. Came in on a big black horse, and nigh took over the place before you could turn and spit.'

'He had plenty of money, then?'

She shrugged. 'As much as he needed. We only had one saloon back in them days, and next thing you knows, Ray Bonny is runnin' it. Then he brings in some of them no-good women, and as the town grew, he opened two more saloons and got hisself on the council. Even tried to get into the territorial legislature at one time. They reckon him as bein' the richest man in Ryker's Ford.'

'So his arrival would be about the last year of the war?'

'I reckon so. This place started movin' when gold was found up on the Gila. And the river-crossin' brought travellers here. We just grewed, and him with it. But he's one bad *hombre*, is Ray Bonny.'

Charlie Finch had a few more talks like that about town and the saloon-keeper heard about it. He went along to see his friend, the marshal.

Bert Warren was alone in his office and rather liked a visit from Ray Bonny. It usually meant a few extra dollars in his pocket, and the marshal of Ryker's Ford was not averse to that. His eyes were alert as the saloon-owner took a seat at the other side of the desk.

'That Pinkerton fella that got killed in the stage

hold-up,' he said slowly, 'did you ever hear any more about him?'

'Sure did,' the marshal said. 'The local agent in Tombstone sent me a letter. Didn't trust the stage or telegraph after what happened. Some fella who was passin' through dropped it in last week.'

'Why the hell didn't you tell me?' the saloon-owner snarled.

'It weren't nothin' to worry you about, Ray,' the marshal whined. 'It's all about some fella by the name of Hudson. Pinkerton's ain't concerned with you. They got this job to look for a missin' fella, and that's what it's all about. I couldn't tell 'em nothing. All we ever saw of him in Ryker's Ford was his hat, and that was twenty years ago.'

Ray Bonny sat playing nervously with the nugget that graced his watch chain.

'There's a fella in town now,' he said, 'and he's askin' questions about me. Name's Charlie Finch and he's stayin' with old Ma Bladon. What do you know about him?'

Bert Warren shrugged. 'He's passin' through on his way to some spread that his son owns near the border, so I'm told. Restin' up for a few days 'cos his horse is kinda tuckered out. I reckon he's just nosy. And he sure don't look like no Pinkerton man to me.'

'That's the trouble, they often don't. Keep an eye on him, Bert. I'll feel happier when he leaves town.'

The marshal ran an uneasy tongue across his badly shaven lips.

'That message I got from the Pinkerton people,' he said quietly, 'they said as how their agent was carryin' a letter to me but that they'd also telegraphed to let me know he was on the way. Sorta playin' safe, you might say.'

'So?'

'Sid Pearson never passed that message on. At least, not to me.'

Ray Bonny leaned across the desk.

'You got a good job here, Bert, and I looks after my friends. Let's just keep it that way.'

He left the office while the marshal looked after his retreating figure with a worried frown on his face.

Ray Bonny rode out of town on his large grey gelding and headed north under the early-morning sun. There was little cloud in the sky and the ground was parched enough to make the noise of hoof-beats almost echo in the still air. He was alert for anybody following and glanced back frequently.

It was two hours before he reached the ridge of rock and the small neat cabin that nestled under it. There was smoke coming from the iron chimney-pipe that stuck out from the wooden walls and stood up above the grass-covered roof. There were two horses grazing close by and the sound of water trickling from a crack in the long sandstone abutment. It was a quiet and peaceful place, off the trail and once used by a family who had been driven from their little spread by poor pasture and not enough rain.

Ray Bonny dismounted and tethered his horse to a rail. He knew that he was being watched from the cabin and called out a greeting as he loosened the animal's girth.

His two gunslingers came out and all three shook hands.

'We've sure been worritted, boss,' one of them said as he led the way inside and poured out some strong coffee. 'It's been a few weeks since we saw you. What's happened to Pete?'

Ray shook his head sadly.

'He never had a chance,' he told them with deep piety. 'The doc did his best, but the wound turned bad and he died in his sleep. That's why I've been lyin' low. We had to bury poor Pete all quiet-like and keep the folks in town thinkin' that nothin' was happening.'

'We'll sure miss him,' the younger man said. 'He was one hell of a hand with a gun.'

They all nodded agreement as they sipped the hot coffee.

'Now we got ourselves a new problem,' Ray said after a while. 'There's a fella in town askin' questions.'

'About us?'

'Yep, and I reckon him for another Pinkerton man. The last one was supposed to be on some other trail, but this coyote keeps bringin' my name up to folks. He's real nosy.'

'You want we should kill him?'

It was the question that Ray Bonny had hoped for.

'It might be just as well,' he said. 'We got a big job comin' our way pretty soon, and the last thing we need is a lawman of any sort watchin' every move. I'll make a show of leavin' town tomorrow noon. He may follow, and if he does, I'll lead him here and you can be up on the ridge waitin' with carbines.'

After a few more minutes of talk, mainly about money, Ray Bonny headed back for town with an easier mind.

FIVE

The saloon-owner came out of the front door of the Lucky Chance and checked the girth of his mount. He was wearing a white trail-coat and carried saddlebags which he threw across the animal's back. He looked up at the sky as if checking the weather, and then gave a wave to the bartender who was brushing the stoop. He swung himself into the saddle to trot quietly up the main street of Ryker's Ford.

He rode with confidence, never glancing back and with his left hand lightly on the rein as the right one rested on his thigh. He was going in the same direction as he had taken the previous day. But he hoped that he was being followed on this occasion.

And he was. Charlie Finch was behind him, riding way back out of sight but following the trail with experience and sureness of eye.

The sandstone ridge came in sight after about two hours. It was hard and dark against the sun.

The little cabin at its base had no smoke coming from the stovepipe and there were no horses in sight. Ray Bonny rode along the base of the ridge, ignoring the cabin and heading steadily towards the north. He looked neither to right nor left and did not see the two Winchester barrels that were pointing down from the rocks above.

They were not aimed at him. They moved round to where Charlie Finch's horse came in view. The two marksmen were some thirty feet apart, about twenty feet from the ground, and with an easy target in their sights. The older one aimed carefully at Charlie's chest, holding his breath as he got ready to pull the trigger.

The shot took him by surprise and he flinched as a spurt of red dust flew up just beyond his left shoulder. He ducked behind the rock as he nearly dropped the carbine in sheer panic.

His companion turned to see what was happening. He was not so lucky. A shot grazed the side of his face and he let out a yell of pain and fear as he let go the Winchester to hear it rattle down to the base of the ridge. He scrambled to his feet, almost blinded by blood as he tried to climb over the top of the rocky ledges and reach his horse at the far side. The other gunslinger was trying to do the same.

Charlie Finch was equally surprised by what was happening. He reined in his mount to look around in bewilderment. The clatter of the carbine as it landed a few yards from him was the only sign of human existence. Ray Bonny had long since vanished from sight and the place seemed deserted.

Charlie drew his own gun and looked up at the ridge for signs of a target. Both riflemen had now crawled their way through the layers of rock to the safety of the far slope where they could reach their tethered horses. As they climbed down amid a scurry of dirt, they were met by two more shots.

Abel Davis had ridden round the end of the ridge and was waiting for them. His carbine was aimed accurately at the older man. The bullet caught him in the chest and he stumbled to his knees. His companion stood uncertainly off his guard and was brought down by the second shot. He staggered up again for a moment and then collapsed in a heap.

In the silence that followed, only the movement of the horses disturbed the air. Two hawks watched from their high perch and a lizard crawled over the gritty sand by Abel Davis's feet. Then Charlie Finch appeared round the corner, his horse on a tight rein as he held a Colt .44 in his right hand, cocked and ready for use.

He stopped as he saw the deputy and the two dead or dying men in front of him. He surveyed the scene calmly and then put the gun away.

'I reckon you saved me from bein' bush-whacked, young fella,' he said quietly. 'I rode right into that one, didn't I?'

Abel Davis lowered his carbine and nodded. There was a slight grin on his face as he approached the man on the horse.

'Ray Bonny led you along nicely, Mr Finch,' he said. 'And I never did trust Ray Bonny.'

'Seems a wise thing to do, fella.'

Charlie Finch got down from his mount and shook hands with the young man.

'I owe you for that,' he said, 'and I figure as how you've been keepin' an eye on things back in Ryker's Ford. What the hell is Bonny up to that concerns the law?'

Abel Davis grinned. 'Well, now that's a long story,' he said. 'There's a cabin back there and I reckon as you and me need some coffee while we talk things over.'

He led the way to the little hut that the bandits had used and threw open the door. The stove was unlit but it took only a short time to set fire to the brushwood that was already laid and get a pot of coffee boiling away. Abel Davis searched the place but found nothing of interest. He poured the drink while the two men faced each other across the table.

'Suppose you tell me what you're doin' in Ryker's Ford, Mr Finch,' the deputy suggested. 'You a Pinkerton man?'

Charlie nodded. 'One of our people was killed a few weeks ago. You heard all about that, of course.

He was on his way to your little town to try and identify a man. Your marshal didn't seem to us to be too trustworthy. Never appeared to get the messages we sent from Tombstone.'

'I ain't claimin' to know all the answers myself,' Abel said as he put down the enamel mug, 'but the marshal takes a few dollars each week from Ray Bonny. And the telegraph man seems to be doin' the same thing. So maybe that puts you on the right track.'

'It sure as hell does. And you?'

The young man grinned. 'I ain't a local, Mr Finch. Just some gunhandler who wants a steady job and landed up here. I reckon as how I'd make a better marshal than Bert Warren, and I got the mayor goin' along with me on that. So where do you fit in?'

'As I told you, I'm here to identify a man. I report back when I've done that and whoever is employin' us can then decide what to do.'

'And you don't know what it's all about?'

'No, but I reckon that Bonny is the man. And that's why he tried to have me bushwhacked.'

'That figures. I followed him to this place once before and I knew them two fellers was workin' for him. I checked the wanted lists back at the jail-house, and the older one is on them. There's a hundred dollars reward for him. Store robberies and rustlin' cattle.'

'And Bonny?'

Abel grimaced. 'He ain't officially done nothin' against the law,' he said. 'He rode out this way, you followed him, but he took no part in the bush-whacking. Just rode straight through. Saw nothin' and heard nothing. I reckon he'll be on his way back to town now as if he'd just been to a church outin' with the choir. He's gonna get one hell of a shock when I get into Ryker's Ford with two dead men across their saddles, and when you show up all safe and healthy.'

'Yeah, it'll be a pleasure to see his face. If I hadn't a job to do, I'd be right anxious to pull a gun on him. What do you aim to be doin' about all this?'

'I figure on sayin' that while I was out lookin' for them stray cattle, I came upon a wanted man. He and another fella was also after the cattle, and we had a shoot-out. Then I collect the reward and my share of the sale of their horses and saddles. I'll tell the mayor what really happened, and leave him to decide what to do next.'

Charlie Finch looked hard at the innocent face of his companion. He knew a shrewd man when he saw one, and he could also spot a ruthless one.

'You do that, fella,' he said. 'I'll be leavin' town in the next day or so to be reportin' back to Tombstone. What do you think the mayor will do about Bonny?'

Abel Davis pulled a face. 'I don't rightly know, but without them two fellas workin' for him, Ray

47

Bonny ain't as big a man as he was. Maybe he'll leave town before we can prove that he was behind the stage hold-ups we've been havin' in the territory.'

'And the killin' of our agent.'

'Yep. He might take fright now.'

'Then I reckon you and me has had a good day, fella.'

Ray Bonny heard the shooting as he rode quietly towards the north for a mile or so before turning back to Ryker's Ford. He was in no hurry and was happy to leave his two colleagues to dispose of the body as arranged. He arrived back in town in the early evening and entered the Lucky Chance through the back door after settling his horse down for the night.

He took a few drinks, cooked himself a meal, then went down to the saloon to see how business was doing. The place was reasonably full for the middle of the week and the faro-table had a few people playing avidly. There was also a good poker-game being controlled by a professional gambler who worked on a commission basis. It was going to be a profitable night and he looked around with a contented air.

Then he saw Charlie Finch.

The Pinkerton man was leaning on the bar with a glass of whiskey in his hand. He seemed calm and cool, as though he had no cares and had not been the victim of a bushwhacking earlier in the day. Ray Bonny's fingers toyed restlessly with the watch-chain as he tried to work out what had gone wrong.

He stood at the bottom of the stairs with his face as set and expressionless as that of the professional poker-player across the room. His mind raced for some explanation. Charlie Finch seemed totally unaware of his presence as he quietly sipped his whiskey and talked to one of the bartenders.

Ray Bonny decided to carry on as though nothing had happened. He went behind the bar, checked the takings, talked to a few regulars, and then went back to stand by the stairs again.

He did not at first notice the entry of a man who pushed through the swing-doors with a look of excitement on his reddened face. There was a sudden rumble of conversation in the room and some of the men began heading for the door. Ray Bonny hesitated. It was plain that something was happening out on the street but he did not wish to be part of an undignified rush.

He walked slowly across the saloon and grabbed one of the men by the arm.

'What's all the fuss about, Harry?' he asked quietly.

'The deputy rode into town with two dead fellas,' the man told him cheerfully. 'Looks like the young lad's been havin' a good day's shooting.'

Ray Bonny's hand began to tremble as he forgot

all about dignity and headed for the door. The street was dark save for the lamplight from the buildings, which threw uneven patterns across the ruts and horse-droppings. There were three animals outside the marshal's office, and dead bodies lay across the saddles of two of them. A crowd was gathering and Ray Bonny watched anxiously as Bert Warren emerged from the jail-house followed by young Abel Davis.

The mayor and a few other prominent citizens were hurrying towards the scene and the saloon-owner decided to join them. He was a councilman and nobody would think it strange if he pushed through the mob to take a close look at the dead men.

He identified them instantly.

Marshal Warren held up a hand to silence the excited crowd.

'Now, folks,' he said with massive solemnity, 'we have here a coupla cattle-thieves who met up with the law once too often. We don't aim to have these sorta fellas around Ryker's Ford, and this is how we deal with 'em. My deputy here, under my orders, went lookin' around the range and caught them dead to rights. I reckon as how he's done a good day's work and the honest folk round here can rest easy, knowin' that they got some law in this town. So we'll just let the mayor take care of the burials before they starts stinkin' up the place.'

Having taken as much credit to himself as possible, the marshal returned to the office while the mayor's assistant started to take away the two horses and their burdens. The crowd began to break up as Ray Bonny looked round to see if Charlie Finch was anywhere in sight. The man was watching him from the doorway of the Lucky Chance.

The Pinkerton man left town the next day just after the departure of the weekly stage. He travelled north towards Tombstone and was quite content at a job completed. He had no real interest in what happened next. He had left a little diversion behind to lull Ray Bonny into a false sense of security, and looked forward to a few days with his family before the company sent him on another job.

The saloon-owner was no tracker but he did manage to follow the man without being seen. He had armed himself with a Winchester and although no expert, was determined to use it. He was more accustomed to having other folk do his killing, and it was a nervous Ray Bonny who waited until Charlie Finch would stop for a noon break. He was banking upon him using a creek that lay on the trail and came from a rocky outcrop where a man might be ambushed as he cooked or ate his midday meal.

When they were nearing the creek the saloon owner spurred his horse to make a wide circling movement so that he would reach the water supply before Charlie. He wanted to lie in wait as near to the creek as possible and get the man with a single shot. It took him more than fifteen minutes to circle round in the hollows and clumps of tall mesquite until he reached the spot where he wanted to be.

The Pinkerton man was still not in sight. He was moving at a slow, easy pace that would not tire his horse. Ray Bonny got his own mare tethered in a clump of bushes and crawled up a slope so that he could look down on the creek. He lay there for a few minutes with the Winchester cocked and lying at his side. He had a clear view of the water and the well-grassed banks on either side of it.

He sweated under the hot sun and the warmth almost made him doze off as he waited, his eyes trying to focus on the heat haze which marked the trail. Then he saw the horseman approaching and breathed a sigh of relief. This was soon followed by a tense feeling of terror in case things went wrong. Ray Bonny was no hero without his gang.

Charlie Finch reached the creek, loosened the girth on his mount, and let it take its fill of water before he tethered it to a clump of tall bushes. He began to gather wood for a fire and unpacked an enamel coffee-pot to make himself a drink. He was feeling relaxed but had enough experience of the trail to know that every sound and movement meant something in the empty wastes of semidesert. He sensed rather than heard that there was another horse nearby.

Ray Bonny's animal could smell the water, and although it did not whinny, its movements were restless as it tugged at the reins and tried to free itself to reach the creek. Its owner was not aware of the slight noises and was fiercely concentrating on the movements of the man he intended to kill.

Charlie Finch poured the coffee-grounds into the heating can, went across to his horse to get some food from one of the saddlebags and was lost from sight for a moment as he moved round the animal's flank. Ray Bonny raised the Winchester to his shoulder and waited for the man to show himself again. He reckoned that the distance was about right and that even if he did not kill with the first shot, it would be enough to tip the scales in his favour.

He waited, but nothing happened. Charlie Finch had vanished. Ray Bonny lowered the gun and an expression of complete puzzlement crept into his sunken eyes. The horse was still there, but its owner seemed to have quietly slipped away through the network of bushes to which the animal was tethered. He uttered a silent curse and slithered backwards down the slope in case he was suddenly taken by surprise.

Ray Bonny was worried now. He was being hunted instead of being the hunter. He rose to his feet at the bottom of the slope and looked around anxiously. The muzzle of his gun moved in slightly shaking arcs as he backed towards his horse.

It was no longer there.

The saloon-owner broke into a cold sweat despite the heat of the day. He was a frightened man and it showed as the gun shook in his hand.

'Drop it.' The voice came from a clump of bushes over to his right. Ray Bonny did as he was told. The cocked Winchester fell from his limp grasp.

Charlie Finch stepped out from the bushes, a shotgun pointed firmly at the startled man. Both hammers were drawn back and at the range between the two opponents, the blast of either barrel would have been devastating.

'Now why would a townsfella like you be followin' a little old country fella like me?' Charlie asked as he took a few paces nearer and beckoned Ray Bonny to back away from the Winchester.

'I was just ridin' through.' It was the best the man could muster on the spare of the moment.

Charlie grinned. 'Is that a fact now?' he asked. 'And you just happened to be lyin' in wait with a carbine pointed at my head? You sure is one strange travellin' fella, Mr Bonny.'

Ray tried to recover some of his poise. His sneer struggled to reassert itself.

'You was spyin' on me back in Ryker's Ford,' he said with a tinge of pious outrage. 'I'm one solid citizen back there and I don't reckon to bein' asked after and followed by some fella from other parts. You can't deny what you been doing, can you?'

'No, you're quite right. I was followin' you. But you turned out to be the wrong fella and so I'm on my way to another job in some other town. You ain't of interest to me no more.'

'Why should I believe that?'

Charlie Finch kept the gun pointed at Ray Bonny while he bent to pick up the Winchester. He flung it far down the slope where it ended up among a pile of brushwood and raised a fine cloud of dust for a moment or two.

'I was told that there was a fella in Ryker's Ford who might be of interest to my agency. I thought at first that you filled the bill. You sure as hell acted suspicious. But I ain't bothering with hold-up men. That's a job for marshals and sheriffs. Once I found what your game really was, I sorta lost interest. As far as I'm concerned, you ain't on my list of important folk no more. So go get your horse and ride back home. I reckon the law will deal with you, one way or another.'

Charlie Finch had already noticed that Ray Bonny carried no holster and had no bulge under his coat that would hide a Colt revolver. He turned on his heel and walked up the slope to get on with his meal before continuing to Tombstone.

But he had underestimated the man. The saloon-owner had a double-barrelled derringer under his waistcoat. He drew the tiny gun rapidly, cocked both barrels, and let fly.

Charlie heard the noise of the hammers going back and was turning around when the shots hit him. He seemed to pause in space for a moment and then crumpled to his knees before sliding down the slope to the feet of the saloon-owner.

'I ain't the trustin' type,' Ray said to the dying man. 'And I ain't takin' no chances on you talkin' about my affairs.'

Ray Bonny rode into Ryker's Ford as quietly and discreetly as he had left it. He was standing at the bar with a cooling glass of beer in his hand when the old man from the telegraph office came in. He got himself a whiskey and then sidled up to the owner.

'I been tryin' to get you all day, Mr Bonny,' he said in a low voice. 'I got somethin' I think you should know.'

'It's no use us talkin' about business now,' the saloon-owner answered tersely. 'We got no guns until Lou Parker can make town with a few friends.'

'Oh, this ain't business, Mr Bonny. It's about that Finch fella what left town this morning. He sent a message to the Pinkerton people in Tombstone.'

Ray Bonny put down his drink and paid more attention. He was feeling scared again.

'What did he have to say?' he asked.

'Just told them that he had been given a wrong steer and there was nothin' at Ryker's Ford to interest the agency. He was goin' back to Tombstone. Is it important?'

Ray Bonny silently cursed himself for the unnecessary dangers that he had endured. The man had been telling him the truth.

'No,' he said glumly. 'It's not important any more.'

SIX

Mayor Ryker listened to the deputy's story without interruption. He nodded occasionally and kept his piggy eyes on the young man's face.

'Well, that sure is some tale,' he said when it was all over. 'So Ray Bonny tried to kill the Pinkerton man and you stopped him dead in his tracks. I gotta hand it to you, fella, you sure as hell make a good lawman. Now we got ourselves a problem.'

'What's that, Mr Mayor?'

'Well, we can't pin anythin' on Bonny. He just rode through like you said and heard nothin' of what was happenin' back at the ridge. So he's still in town, carryin' on as normal. But at least he ain't got no back-up no more. The stages will be safe until he gets another gang together. But what about this Finch fella? You say he's left town. Ain't he got no more interest in Bonny?'

Abel Davis shrugged his shoulders.

'Didn't say much one way or another,' he answered. 'Just said he'd report back and went off this morning. Followed the stage out, but he weren't gallopin' away like they was.'

The young man leaned over the rather smelly table on which many dead bodies had lain in the mortician's parlour.

'Charlie Finch seemed more interested in that Hudson fella than in anythin' that's happenin' these days. He was lookin' at them photo things in the Lucky Chance saloon. And he was askin' about things that Ray Bonny might have been involved in when he first came to Ryker's Ford. Well, that's nigh on eighteen or twenty years ago, so they tell me. Do you understand it, Mr Mayor?'

'Not really, but I recall as how some ranchers brought in the hat they'd found with the name of Hudson inside it. We never had no marshal or mayor in them days. My old pa was more or less runnin' the place. There weren't nothin' anybody could do, and nobody had ever heard tell of a fella named Hudson, so the whole thing just died out. I reckon as how Ray Bonny arrived in town around that time with a load of money and an eye to make more. Maybe he and Hudson had some sorta fallin'-out and Hudson got treated the way Charlie Finch was meant to go. Our saloon-keeper ain't no nice fella.'

The mayor stood up and straightened his waist-coat.

'And talkin' of nice fellas,' he said, 'that tele-graph-operator needs a little lesson on how to stay healthy in my town. You go keep the marshal quiet while I have a word in Sid Pearson's ear.'

The two men parted and the mayor went through to the back room where his assistant was preparing the dead bandits for burial. He checked that the cheapest possible job was being done and then put on his hat and walked down the main street to the telegraph office.

Sid Pearson was at his desk, making some entries in his log-book and smoking a corncob pipe that filled the place with vile fumes. The mayor pulled up an old bentwood chair and sat down opposite the surprised man.

'Now, Sid,' he said in a friendly voice, 'you and me has to have a little understanding.'

The man blinked and wiped a watery eye.

'Somethin' wrong, Mr Mayor?' he asked uneasily.

'Yes, there is in a way. You see, the telegraph is an important thing to a town like this, and we gotta make sure that it ain't used for any purpose other than what's legal and decent. Do you follow me?'

There was a slight tremor in the operator's hand as he put down his pen.

'I reckon so, Mayor,' he said slowly, 'but all I do is send and receive messages. The line ain't used for nothin' else.'

'It's what happens to the messages that concerns me, Sid,' Mayor Ryker said grimly.

'Now if you're talkin' about the message that

never reached the marshal about that visitin'
Pinkerton man, I didn't get that signal. I told Bert
Warren when he came askin' around. Y'see, there
are times when the line goes off 'cos somebody
shoots out an insulator or a flock of birds is settlin'
on the wires and makin' it all of a jumble. These
things happen now and then.'

'I'm sure they do, Sid, but I ain't as trustin' as
the marshal. I did me some checkin' with the
senders in Tombstone. A mayor's got some
almighty pull when it comes to gettin' information
like that. The message got sent here allright, and
you acknowledged receivin' it loud and clear. You
just never got around to showin' it to the marshal.'

There was a long silence while the telegraph
man swallowed and put his pipe down on the desk.

'I musta made some sorta mistake, Mr Mayor,'
he managed to say after a while.

'You did. As I see it, you went along to Ray
Bonny, showed him the message, and then
destroyed it at his orders. It said that a Pinkerton
man was comin' into town and would be carryin' a
letter to Bert Warren, detailin' his investigation.
The help of the law was bein' asked for and the
telegraph message was confirmin' his arrival on
the stage. Ray Bonny was scared as hell, wasn't he,
Sid?'

The man gulped noisily.

'Yeah, well, I reckon as how you're gonna have
me out of a job, and I never did expect a killin' to

61

be done. So here goes. It was Ray Bonny. He pays me a few dollars to keep an eye on any messages that might concern him. I never meant no harm, Mr Mayor, but I got a wife and she's ailin' somethin' bad these days.'

'I know, Sid.' The mayor nodded his head sympathetically. 'And I don't aim to see you in trouble if it can be helped. Ray Bonny is a dangerous man, and if he asks a fella to do something, it's hard to say no. But you and me gotta have an understandin' about this. Agreed?'

'Whatever you say, Mr Mayor.'

'Well now, any more messages that come through the wire and concern Ray Bonny, you let him have them, just as you do now. But with one slight difference. You also tell me.'

'And the marshal?'

'No, just me. I ain't figurin' on interferin' with Bonny's private business matters, but I want tellin' about everythin' that comes over that mess of wires. You got that?'

'I got it, Mr Mayor,' the man said eagerly. 'You can depend on me.'

'I'd better. You just do that and your job's safe. But remember, Sid. If you let me down in any way, you not only lose your job here, but you'll likely end up in the territory jail. And that ain't nice for a man of your age and with an ailin' wife and all.'

Sid Pearson kept his promise and a few days later

he knocked quietly on the back door of the funeral parlour. He was admitted by an aproned mayor who was now in his capacity as a mortician. Old Ma Gurning had died and was being set up for a very profitable funeral.

'I just had a message from Tombstone,' the man said eagerly. 'Charlie Finch has not turned up there and his office want to know if he's still in town.'

'What did you answer?' the mayor asked as he peeled off his cotton gloves and apron.

'I said that he left on the same day as the stage and that I myself saw him headin' outa town behind it. I also said I'd check around and ask the marshal. But I comes to you first.'

Mayor Ryker nodded.

'You did quite right, Sid. You go tell Bert Warren all about it while I ask around town.'

After Sid Pearson had scurried away, the mayor put on his coat and went along to the Wells Fargo office. The clerk was labelling some parcels and looked up from his work at the rare sight of a visit from the mayor.

'When you was seein' the stage off to Tombstone the other day,' the First Citizen asked in an official-sounding voice, 'did you notice a fella who rode outa town at the same time? On an old mare with a shotgun and a coupla saddlebags.'

'Charlie Finch?' the clerk asked as he stuck the pen behind his ear. 'Sure. He came to this office and hung around for a while. I reckon he was up to no good.'

'What do you mean?'

'Well, Mr Mayor, some folks tries to save money by not usin' our services properly. So they slips a letter to some passenger they think they can trust. I figure that's what he did. I sure saw him hand somethin' to a fella what was travellin' to Tombstone.'

'Has anybody else been askin' about Charlie Finch?' the mayor asked.

The man shook his head.

'Right, then let's keep this between ourselves,' Mayor Ryker cautioned him. 'Charlie Finch has gone missin' so it's a matter for the law. Not for saloon gossip.'

He left the offended Wells Fargo man and returned to his office with the knowledge that Charlie Finch had got his report through even if he never got back to Tombstone himself.

SEVEN

Ray Bonny left town a week later. He took the stage to Tombstone and travelled as any other passenger would have done, armed with a carpetbag and a clear conscience. The mayor, the marshal, his deputy, and the telegraph operator all watched him go. Each was left with his own thoughts on the matter.

He returned a few days later, looking as gaunt as ever and sneering as usual. He entered the Lucky Chance saloon with his normal confident stride to check the books and look around for faults. He then retired to his quarters for a meal and a refreshing drink. Ray Bonny had done what he set out to do. He had met up with Lou Parker and arranged another meeting when the man had got some more guns together who would take orders from a boss behind the scenes and raid the stage without argument. The saloon-owner was getting back into his favourite business.

Marshal Warren showed no interest. While life

was quiet and food and drink were plentiful, he was a happy man. Ray Bonny was the last person he would spy on or worry about. He just ignored the man's activities as much as he ignored his own suspicions.

Abel Davis watched more eagerly. He had noted every movement that Ray Bonny had made and was waiting for him to leave town for some new meeting when he'd got a gang together again. The deputy had no doubt that it would happen. With the Pinkerton Agency not interested in the man, he was free to start up again and would always remain in the background so that no real evidence would put him in front of a judge.

Abel and the mayor were waiting patiently. A message would come through on the telegraph sooner or later and Ray Bonny would leave town to contact his new gang. Then a stage would be raided. But with one difference. They would get the message at the same time as Bonny, and would be able to telegraph the authorities wherever the raid was likely to take place. The gang would be caught and one of them would be sure to talk.

Old Sid Pearson listened in to all the messages that passed along the line. He heard everything and knew that he had to play it safe if he wanted to survive. The man was scared but he also realized that if Ray Bonny was caught, it was a hanging matter for the saloon-owner and he would not be able to take revenge on the telegraph operator.

Just over a week after Ray Bonny got back to Ryker's Ford things began to happen. A man rode into town one warm, windless afternoon and tethered his horse outside the Lucky Chance saloon. He was a big man, dark and grim-faced, with thick black brows which met above his prominent nose. He carried two guns at his waist and a newish Winchester rested in the holster against the saddle of his large black gelding. Everything about the man gave an impression of darkness and power. He dusted his shoulders and chest with a gloved hand and entered the saloon.

There were only a few drinkers there so early in the day, and the gaming-tables stood deserted. Two bartenders were talking and they glanced up at the new arrival. One of them muttered something and then headed for the stairs to alert the owner.

'Whiskey.'

The newcomer's voice was deep and hoarse, and he took the drink without thanks. His glance circled the room and then rested on the stairs as if waiting for something to happen. It soon did. Ray Bonny came slowly down with his hand tapping the rail as he moved silently on the thick carpet. He came across to stand at the side of the visitor.

'I told you to come round the back, Lou,' he said in a taut voice.

'I don't go sneakin' round like some frightened gopher,' the big man told him bluntly. 'Just get your horse and take me out to this place you have in mind.'

Ray Bonny fought back his anger.

'Where have you left the others?' he demanded in a low voice. 'I hope you've brought them as you promised. We need to get settled in ready for business when the chance comes up.'

'They're out on the trail and not gettin' any richer while we stand here gabbin' about it. Let's move outa this place before folks wake up enough to notice a stranger and start askin' me to join the preacher's choir.'

Ray Bonny cursed under his breath and led the way to the back room of the building.

'Stay here while I saddle up,' he ordered, 'and then go round to collect your own horse. I'll wait by the corral for you and we'll go pick up your men. Then it's only an hour from here so you'll soon be settled in for the night. I'll be back here before anyone really misses me. I've picked a place we've not used before. There's food and beddin' there, and a small creek a few yards away. There's no stove but you can light a fire outside without anyone seein' the smoke. The place is well off the trail and there's no cattle grazin' nearby.'

He turned to go but the other man caught him by the arm and swung him round.

'How long are we gonna have to wait at this place?' he asked.

'I don't know,' the saloon-owner answered impatiently. 'But we've got to be ready when word comes through. I just hope these fellas you've hitched up with know what they're doing.'

'They'll take their orders from me, but none of us aims to hang around in some damp cabin till we die of old age.'

Ray Bonny shook off the arm and went out to get his horse saddled. The two men were on their way a few minutes later. They travelled north at first, stopping a short way out of town to pick up Lou Parker's two companions.

They were both young men, slim and poorly dressed, who looked like out-of-work cowpokes. Their animals were small but sturdy and the riders greeted Lou and Ray Bonny with clear relief on their immature faces. Both carried Winchesters and each had a Colt pistol of matching calibre at his belt.

They headed south-west now, towards the border, travelling over rough ground where the wind had eroded the soil and exposed coloured rocks that shone in the late sunlight. There was little grass and the only creatures were lizards which scurried over the hot ground. A haze covered the distant landscape to hide the low hills that had once been tree-lined until loggers had cut everything down to sell to the Confederate armies.

The little group reached its goal in slightly less than an hour. It was a log-cabin, solidly built but lacking glass for the single window. The tree-fellers had once used it, but that was more than twenty years ago. It was clean enough inside and Ray Bonny had made a few quiet trips from town to make sure that there were blankets, food, and plenty of candles to make the place as comfortable as possible.

He saw the men settled in and then went back to his own horse. Lou Parker accompanied him and stood silently as the saloon-owner tightened the girth and prepared to mount.

'We'll hear from you soon, then?' Lou prompted.

'As soon as possible. I gotta rely on other people to feed me information, so don't let them fellas loose in town to do any drinkin' or whoring. It could spoil a good set-up. We've got somethin' big goin' here and there's no point in messin' it up for the sake of whiskey or women.'

Lou nodded impatiently.

'I'll keep them in order,' he promised, 'but they won't like the thought of you takin' half the money and stayin' at home while they're out takin' all the risks.'

'The last raid we did brought in seven thousand dollars from a lumber company payroll,' Ray Bonny said bluntly. 'Half of that divided between three fellas is worth a bit of a risk. And just remember this. Without me, you got nothin' at all. The three of you was rustlin' a few cattle and riskin' a lynch-mob. With this set-up, I get the word, tell you

70

the best place to hold up the stage, and we all make a few dollars. So just tell them overgrown kids that we ain't playin' for a handful of candies. This is a big game and it's worth a few risks.'

'You never did tell me what happened to your last gang,' Lou said tersely. 'Them fellas in there ain't got my trustin' nature. What do I tell them if they ask that question?'

'You can tell them the truth and they might take heed of it. One of them was wounded in a hold-up and died of his injuries. The other two was hidin' out, just like you are, but they got greedy and went off stealin' cattle. A local deputy caught up with them and they had a cheap funeral back in town.'

He mounted his horse and rode off before his colleague could pose any more awkward questions. Lou Parker returned to the cabin where the two young men had lit a candle to add a little light to the fading afternoon sun. They had some food unpacked and were looking to him for guidance.

'You can build a fire outside,' he told them, 'and Ray says that the creek is down the slope just behind this place. But before we do any of that, I got somethin' to say, so listen.'

They both nodded silently. He stood with his back to the open doorway, eyeing them sternly.

'Ray Bonny says as how we're not to go into town in case the locals get suspicious. That makes sense, but I got me a slightly different idea. We cross the border into Mexico, steal a few horses, and then come back here with them. When we hold up this stage for him, we use the Mexican animals, and we all have beards. So start growin' them now.'

The paler of the two youths stroked his hairless chin.

'I don't have much in the way of whiskers, Lou,' he said ruefully.

'No, I reckon not, so you rub dirt round your face. The idea is that the folk robbin' the stage have got to be as different to us as we can make them. Three bearded fellas on Mexican horses, and maybe even with Mexican saddles is what they'll see. That's a hell of a lot different to three well-turned-out gents in nice clean shirts ridin' on cow-ponies. We'll cover our faces in the raid but the beards will show just a little and we may even be able to pick up some of them Mexican hats while we're across the border.'

The other two grinned at the thought and the beardless one put a question.

'How does Mr Bonny know when a stage is carryin' cash?' he asked.

Lou Parker viewed him with a certain respect.

'That's a question I been askin' myself,' he admitted after a pause. 'And I'd sure as hell like to know the answer. He could get a message from somebody in one of the Wells Fargo offices, or from some bankin' fella in another town. Could even be a stage-driver or a guard. There's one hell of a lotta folk will take money off a man as rich as he is. But I'd like to know the answer, all the same. If we knew that, we wouldn't need to give him half the money no more. So think about it when we dresses nice and goes into Ryker's Ford for a coupla quiet drinks and a call on a few lively ladies.'

He looked from one to the other and could tell from the expressions on their faces that they agreed with him.

'In the meantime,' he said cheerfully, 'we light a fire, have a meal, and get some sleep before makin' a trip across the border early in the morning.'

EIGHT

The stage was travelling at a steady pace and the clouds of yellow dust marked its trail for the best part of a mile. They were two hours out from the last change of horses and well on time in the dry weather. There were four passengers, all men, and all dozing fitfully in the swaying vehicle.

The guard and driver talked in a desultory way as they sped across the open areas, but going through gulches or places where bushes of any sort grew, was a different matter. The guard would tighten his grip on the shotgun and look almost nervously around until they were in open space again with a clear field of vision on all sides.

Bedford Creek was the most dangerous spot. The ridges of pale rock grew up on either side of the trail where the creek broke out and formed a pool of clear water that gradually vanished again a few hundred yards out on the flatter ground. There were plenty of mesquite bushes there and a stunted sycamore. Birds and other creatures gathered around the welcome oasis. The guard was tensely alert as they thundered through the narrowed trail and past the flow of water. He only relaxed when they were in the open again.

But he relaxed too soon.

The left front wheel suddenly hit a newly dug pothole which had been hidden by brushwood. The stage lumbered over with a sickening jolt that woke the passengers and nearly threw the guard from his seat. He lost his grip on the shotgun and it flew over the side of the rig to land at the edge of the trail. The driver managed to control the horses in their panic at suddenly being unable to pull a dead weight that tightened their harness as he tugged at the reins.

Three horsemen appeared from behind the stage. They had been hidden among the mesquite, waiting to lure the driver and guard into a false sense of security after leaving Bedford Creek. One of the horsemen fired and the driver leapt up in his seat before toppling off the rig while the reins fell loose between the flanks of the horses. The guard struggled to control his own slide from the seat and went for the Colt at his waist. Another shot took him in the neck and he slumped down.

One horseman appeared at each door of the stage and guns were pointed at the passengers through the windows.

'Just keep it calm, *amigos*, we ain't got nothin' against you,' one of the horsemen shouted.

The passengers did as they were told and sat looking at the men on their small Mexican ponies. It was not possible to identify any of them. Bandannas covered their faces and only exposed a trace of beard. The man who spoke had a strange accent and his saddle was a large Mexican type with small silver studs mounted among the leather-work. All three wore sombreros which had once been white but were now a dirty grey.

One of the bandits climbed up on the seat, pushed the injured guard out of the way, and reached down for the strongbox. He threw it to the ground and then climbed down again to mount his pony with the box across the saddle bow. There was a triumphant shout in Spanish and the three men rode off in a cloud of dust. The passengers breathed a sigh of relief as they heard them disappearing into the distance.

Mayor Ryker walked down the main street with a confident air. He acknowledged the folk who bade him a good morning, and he smiled affably as he entered the office of his cousin, the marshal of Ryker's Ford.

'A lovely day, Bert,' he greeted the surprised lawman. 'And I bring you good news.'

Bert Warren looked up from the cup of coffee and viewed his visitor warily.

'Is that a fact now?' he murmured. 'You buryin' some rich fella what wants all the trimmings and a heavenly choir?'

The mayor sat down opposite the desk and looked around.

'You will have your little joke, Bert,' he said cheerfully. 'Where's your deputy?'

'Takin' his breakfast, I reckon. There isn't a lot of work for the young fella to do. I keep a peaceful town here.'

The mayor smiled.

'True,' he agreed. 'Now, how would you like to collect a sizeable reward, get your picture in the Tombstone papers, and be the hero of Ryker's Ford?'

The marshal's eyes narrowed.

'What are you gettin' at, Steve?' he asked. 'You been drinkin' embalmin' fluid?'

'Take that hold-up the other day. Three fellas got away with the loggin' company payroll up near Bedford Creek. You heard about it, of course?'

'Sure. I got it on the telegraph. It ain't in my territory though. It's for the County folks to worrit about. Six thousand dollars or more, weren't it?'

'That's right, and a five-hundred-dollar reward. And that reward is all yours.'

The marshal's eyes opened wide.

'And how do you figure that out?' he asked.

'Because I know where the hold-up fellas is hidin' out.'

The marshal sat back in his chair and looked hard and long at his cousin. He could see the look on the man's face and realized that this was not some kind of joke.

'You'd better explain yourself, Steve,' he said slowly. 'This is quite a surprise you're handin' me.'

The mayor leaned forward across the desk and spoke in a low voice.

'A man in my job picks up a lotta hints and gossip,' he said, 'and most of it goes in one ear and out the other. But just now and then, there's a grain of truth in it. Somebody in this town is behind that hold-up, and all the other stage attacks in the last few years. I think I know who it is, and I think you know too. Do we understand each other?'

The marshal suddenly lost interest in the reward and his face became a taut mask.

'I don't know what the hell you're talkin' about,' he muttered.

'Bert, you've taken a weekly pay-off from a certain person for a good many years. You've ignored his crooked gamblin' and all his other activities. I don't blame you. A marshal's pay ain't up to much. But things have changed and he's on the way out. You've got to decide where you stand, Bert. It's either him or me. You stick with him, and you go when he goes. You stick with me and I'll see you retire with a bit of ready money and a nice little job that will bring in a few extra dollars. So?'

The marshal sat silently for a few moments.

'So Ray Bonny's finished then?' he asked quietly.

'Dead as the folk I bury every day.'

'He's got three saloons and a few other interests around town, and no kin,' Bert Warren said slowly. 'What happens to all them things?'

'Well, I'm the mayor, and you're the marshal. The judge is a friend, and he knows how to sort out the legal side of things. So I reckon we can all end up a few dollars richer.'

The lawman cheered up at the thought.

'So what have you got in mind?' he asked.

'That young fella that works for me is keepin' watch at what happens at the Lucky Chance,' Mayor Ryker said slowly. 'Them fellas raided the stage two days back and it would take them about that much time to get to the hide-out that they're using. That means they should get there some time tonight. My guess is that Ray Bonny will be headin' out to get his share of what they took. Then we have all four of them together.'

He did not think it wise to mention that the deputy marshal had been his main helper and that the young fellow from the burial parlour was just roped in when necessary.

'And we go out there with a posse?' the marshal asked as he took in the words. 'Round 'em up and bring them back to town for trial?'

'Not exactly.' The mayor shook his head. 'It's more complicated than that, Bert. They'd be brought to trial in a territorial court. They ain't committed no crimes in this town. And that means that with smart-ass lawyers tellin' the tale, we would-n't be able to control things. Bonny has money, and he knows how to spend it. If he got off, or was allowed to escape, there are plenty of folk round here who would look on him as some sort of hero. No, Bert. When that posse attacks the cabin where these fellas is holed up, nobody comes out alive.'

The marshal's mouth opened wide and his hands began to tremble slightly.

'But we gotta call on them to give up,' he protested. 'It ain't proper to go shootin' folk down. I'm a lawman, Steve.'

'Bert. Can you afford to have Ray Bonny tellin' his tale in a court? Does either of us want him to have time to make some sort of arrangements for disposin' of his saloons? Think about it, fella.'

Marshal Warren sat low in his chair and rocked it gently back and forth as he nervously considered his position.

'And I get the reward?' he asked cautiously.

'You do, and all the credit. But there'll be no reward and damn all credit if Bonny goes spoutin' about payin' off the marshal of Ryker's Ford every week.'

The posse was gathered at the west end of the town. They were well away from the darkened buildings and all eight of them were sitting their restless mounts in a little dip in the ground that hid them from sight. The marshal was armed with shotgun, Winchester, and an air of command that he had never before demonstrated. His deputy was at his side as they waited silently under a clouded night sky with only a vague trace of a moon that was hidden for most of the time.

A bat soared across the face of one of the horses and there was a moment of tension. Another animal stamped its hoof as a scorpion started to crawl over its fetlock. Nerves were on edge and the sudden appearance of the mayor came as a relief from the waiting.

'He set out about ten minutes ago,' Steve Ryker told the marshal quietly. 'He's wearin' a white trail-coat and ridin' that big horse of his so we don't need to follow too closely. Young Abel knows where their hideout is so it's easy to follow him. I told your deputy the location to save time while you were gettin' the posse together.'

The marshal nodded. He doubted the honesty of the part that his deputy had played, but he had to be content and do as the mayor commanded.

'Right, off you go,' the mayor ordered. 'And remember, Bert, this is one time you don't bring 'em back alive.'

'I thought you were comin' with us,' the lawman said bleakly.

'Ain't proper for the mayor to go ridin' posse. I know I can leave it all to you, fella. Now don't tell this lot that Ray Bonny is involved. Let them find out for themselves. Good luck.'

81

The mayor departed as swiftly as he had appeared and Marshal Warren set off in the direction that Abel Davis indicated.

They rode in silence under an improving sky. The moon came through more often to light up the trail while Abel Davis rode ahead to make sure that they did not catch up with Ray Bonny and alert him to the trap that had been laid.

The young deputy had been watching events for days. He had taken his orders from the mayor but was surprised when Steve Ryker had told him that there was a change of plans. They would not alert the territorial authorities when the telegraph operator tipped them off about a money shipment. They would let the hold-up take place and catch Ray Bonny at the cabin taking part in the share-out. It would be more conclusive, and there would be no escape route for the saloon-owner. Abel Davis was quite content. It made sense.

There was one moment during the ride when he caught sight of Ray Bonny's gaunt figure ahead. The man's white trail-coat reflected the light of the moon and his large grey gelding was unmistakable. The deputy rode back to the main body and had them wait a few minutes until the man was out of sight and hearing.

The cabin was showing a light around the edges of the window and the door when they reached it. The steady glow was of an oil-lamp rather than candlelight, and some sacking had been drawn across the window to keep out the wind and the insects. There were horses in the corral and Ray Bonny's large animal was tethered to the rail outside the cabin. Voices could be heard inside and the marshal lay on his large stomach at the edge of a slope, looking down on the scene. He was sweaty with the exertion and the prospect of a shoot-out.

'We got 'em dead to rights,' he murmured to Abel Davis. 'Go back there and tell the fellas to take up positions all round, and to open fire when I give the word. And don't forget, we don't know that Bonny is one of the gang.'

The deputy nodded and slipped backwards down the rear side of the slope to join the other six men who had dismounted and drawn their carbines.

He told them what to do and added a warning of his own.

'Shoot to kill,' he advised. 'These fellas are in for a hangin' and they're not goin' to be fussy about shootin' us. They've already taken a few lives and they'll fight like hell.'

'They're better dead,' one of men muttered savagely. 'If we go sendin' them to the courts, a pack of crooked lawyers could get them off.'

The others nodded their agreement and the posse began to group round the cabin as silently as they could. Abel went back to crouch down next to the marshal.

'Any signs?' he asked.

'Not yet, but I figure on shootin' as soon as they opens that door to let Ray Bonny out. If we get him first, the rest will be easy.'

It was the best part of twenty minutes before the door opened noisily and light flooded out onto the well-trodden open space in front of the cabin. Two figures appeared in the gap, one in a white trail-coat and the other a large man in tight black shirt, leather waistcoat, and two guns at his belt.

The marshal raised the Winchester to his shoulder and took careful aim. Ray Bonny was his target and he knew that he could not afford to miss.

The shot echoed across the empty space and was followed almost instantly by a hail of bullets from the other members of the posse. The two men at the doorway dropped in their tracks. Bonny's horse shied and broke free from its tether. It moved a few yards before collapsing from a bullet wound in the head. The door of the cabin started to close but was partially blocked by the fallen bodies. Somebody began pulling them into the hut but the shooting was too heavy. The door stayed ajar as the light went out and the whole place fell into darkness.

There was a lull for a moment or two as the posse reloaded their guns and the fallen horse kicked wildly in its last throes. Abel Davis ran towards the cabin, ducking low and trying to approach at a wide angle that would make a shot from the window as difficult as possible. He managed to reach the safety of the side wall and hugged the rough logs closely as he moved round the corner until he was near the window.

He could hear voices inside. They were whispering and it was not possible to make out any words. The window with its flapping piece of sacking was only a foot above his head as he bent low. He carried a shotgun and quietly pulled back both hammers ready for use. As the rest of the posse watched from their various positions, he suddenly straightened up and emptied both barrels through the window.

They were wild shots but he heard yells of pain or fright as he dropped the empty gun to run to the door. He kicked it back and had his Colt .44 drawn and cocked as he entered the little cabin. He did not need it. One of the men was lying across the table with part of his face blown away. The other knelt almost hidden in a corner, clutching his chest and almost dead from the bleeding of the devastating shotgun blast at close range.

Abel Davis went back to the door and called on the posse to join him. Marshal Warren was first on the spot. He edged round the two bodies in the doorway and then looked at the others in the cabin. He was as anxious as the mayor not to have anyone alive who might know too much, and talk too much. The deputy found the oil-lamp and lit it again. It shone a gentle light over the money that lay on the table in three small heaps. The strong-box was on the floor with a broken hasp.

Marshal Warren went across to the figure in the white trail-coat that lay face down with a pool of blood gathering around it. He thrust his hands into the deep pockets and pulled out a white cotton bag. It was the other half of the payroll cash. Everything had been recovered and the lawman would be the hero of Ryker's Ford and richer by a decent reward.

'Well, I reckon as how we've done a good job here,' Bert Warren said cheerfully. 'We'll put these fellas across their horses and take everythin' back to town. We'll sure as hell be on a lotta free drinks tomorrow night.'

One of the posse was examining the faces of the two dead men in the doorway.

'I know one of these fellas,' he said slowly. 'Seen him in Ryker's Ford, I have.'

'Is that a fact?' The marshal winked at Abel Davis as they watched the man bending across the corpse in the white trail-coat. 'And who would it be then?'

'It's one of them fellas from the Lucky Chance saloon. I think he's called Abe Lawson and he tends bar there.'

NINE

'And the fella even stole my horse?'

Ray Bonny shook his head at the dishonesty of the human race. He sat in the mayor's office with several other members of the council while the marshal stood with young Abel Davis as interested spectators.

'So it would appear,' the mayor said drily. 'And your trail coat as well.'

'And was he the fella behind all them hold-ups?' the saloon-owner asked in wonderment. 'I just can't believe it.'

'Neither can I,' the mayor replied, 'but that's the way it'll have to go down on the record. All the money was recovered and the territorial people are satisfied. Marshal Warren here gets the reward, and the town has to pay posse money and bury the dead.'

Ray Bonny gave them all the benefit of one of his sneers.

'Seems to have worked well enough then,' he said cheerfully. 'But I'm out one good horse.'

'So you are, but you got your trail coat back and one of the girls at Ma Grant's whore house can patch up the holes for you.'

Ray Bonny looked hard at the mayor and even harder at the two lawmen. He took a sip at the whiskey and muttered something about getting back to his work. The others were silent as he left the office and crossed through the room where the four dead men lay ready for burial. He never bothered to glance at Lou Parker but just nodded to the mortician's young helper as he went out on the street to stalk angrily towards the Lucky Chance saloon.

The mayor poured more drinks and looked round the assembled councilmen.

'I hope you fellas realize what's happened here,' he said savagely. 'That crafty coyote sent somebody else to collect the money while he stayed safely in town. He's the one behind all these hold-ups, and he's laughin' fit to bust at us.'

'I'm not sure I can go along with that,' Banker Stanley said slowly. 'Ray Bonny may be a hard man but I don't see him as a gang leader. He's a respected citizen, and one of us.'

'And a damned good customer at your bank,' the mayor snapped.

'That ain't fair. You're all customers at my bank, and I got no special treatment for one more than the other. Let's not judge so hastily, Steve, lest we be judged.'

Mayor Ryker snorted.

'Lookit, you psalm-singin' panty-waist,' he bawled angrily. 'There's more happenin' in this town than you know of, and Ray Bonny is back of it. Ain't that right, Marshal?'

The question took Bert Warren by surprise but he managed to nod his head vigorously. He had burned his boats with the saloon-owner and had to support the mayor now.

'It sure is, Mr Mayor,' he agreed hastily. 'And we figured we had him dead to rights back at that cabin.'

'Exactly,' his cousin said, 'and now I'll tell this meetin' somethin' that we've been keepin' quiet about until there was more proof.'

He turned to the flustered banker.

'But I got a question to ask you first, Len, and I want a straight answer for the good of this town. How much money did Ray Bonny have when he first came here?'

Banker Stanley's babyish face flushed even more as he pursed his little lips in horror.

'These matters are private, Steve,' he protested. 'I don't go talkin' about your account and we got no rights. . . !'

'The law's got some rights,' the mayor snapped, 'and the decent folk of Ryker's Ford have some rights. Ray Bonny turned up here about twenty years ago, didn't he?'

The banker nodded glumly. He looked at the other councilmen but could find no sympathy in their faces.

'Yes,' he agreed glumly. 'About then.'

'And came with a heap of money. Am I right?'

'Yes.'

'So where did he get it?'

'I don't ask my customers questions like that,' the banker said with an attempt at defiance. 'Half the people in this town would run for cover if I did.'

'That's true enough,' one of the councilmen agreed with a laugh.

The mayor glared him down.

'At about the time Ray Bonny arrived in town,' he said grimly, 'some horse-traders came to Ryker's Ford with a hat that had a name inside it. It apparently belonged to a fella called Hudson. They said that they found it up on the trail near Mungo Creek. It weren't called Mungo Creek in them days, but that was where these fellas said they found it. My pa was runnin' the town then and we had no lawman or mayor. So nobody paid much heed to it. We just kept the hat at the ferry cabin in case somebody claimed it or came lookin' for a man named Hudson. But nobody ever did and it was forgot.'

He looked round the attentive faces and knew that he had his audience.

'Until that Pinkerton man was killed on the stage,' he said slowly. 'He was lookin' for a fella called Hudson, and that's why Ray Bonny's men raided that stage. They destroyed letters addressed to the marshal, and made sure that there were no survivors. Now, don't that tell you somethin' about our upright citizen?'

'Are you sure about this?' the banker asked softly. 'It's a mighty serious charge you're making, Steve.'

'I'm sure. Pinkerton's sent out another man, and he never got back to Tombstone. He left here safe enough, but he ain't been heard of since. And this young fella here will tell you that them two rustlers he shot was workin' for Ray Bonny and was tryin' to kill the Pinkerton man. Is that right, son?'

Abel Davis nodded.

Banker Stanley leaned forward across the table and they could all see that he was ready to tell them what he knew.

'Ray Bonny arrived here with eleven thousand dollars,' he said. 'It was the biggest bundle of money I'd ever handled in Ryker's Ford. We'd only just opened for business and that was one hell of a boost for my reputation back at headquarters. I didn't ask no questions. There was a war on and folk were movin' money around fit to bust.'

'Confederate dollars?' someone asked eagerly.

'Hell, no. Yankee dollars. That's another reason I kept quiet about it. A lotta folk around here was supportin' the South, and a man with Yankee dollars was a suspicious character.'

'In more ways than one,' the mayor said with grim satisfaction.

'But what's that got to do with this Hudson fella?' the banker asked.

'Well, now there you got me,' the mayor admitted. 'The Pinkerton men were checkin' on Ray Bonny and askin' about this other mysterious stranger who lost his hat at Mungo Creek. But suppose he lost somethin' else at Mungo Creek? His life.'

There was a long silence as the mayor sat watching the faces of the other men in the room. He knew that he was making an impression but wanted one of them to take up the running.

'Are you suggesting,' asked banker Stanley, 'that Ray Bonny and this Hudson fella was in cahoots in some crooked deal, and that they had a fallin' out?'

'Could be,' the mayor replied calmly. 'And Hudson got hisself killed to leave Bonny rich enough to finish the journey to Ryker's Ford and make you a happy man with all them lovely Yankee dollars.'

'I never did like the fella,' one of the councilmen said piously.

The others nodded agreement while they all ignored the amount of time they had spent in his saloons and whorehouse.

'So what do we do now?' asked the banker.

'Now that's the problem,' the mayor said with genuine sorrow. 'We got nothin' on him. There ain't a bit of real evidence we can take to court, and not a witness alive.'

'What will the Pinkerton people do?' the marshal asked. 'I ain't heard another word out of them.'

'They'll do nothin' unless someone pays them to follow it up,' the mayor said bluntly. 'They've lost two men and they're not in the business of doin' a lawman's job unless somebody foots the bill. Their last agent here was Charlie Finch, and he sent a telegraph message to Tombstone to tell them that he was on a wrong steer. That means they got no interest in our town and we have to handle this among ourselves. Any ideas?'

There were uneasy looks round the table, but nobody had an answer. Ray Bonny was too rich, too powerful, and the sort of figure that scared most of the councilmen.

'We gotta act lawful,' the mayor said, 'and that means we gotta wait for the next move he makes. We have one hope in all this. Charlie Finch gave a letter to some fella travellin' to Tombstone. I'm bettin' my poke on that letter bein' sent to the Pinkerton people to tell them a few things he didn't put in his telegraph message.'

'So another Pinkerton fella might come to town after all?' the banker asked a little glumly. He could see himself losing a good customer.

'I reckon so,' Mayor Ryker grinned. 'Ray Bonny's troubles might just be startin' all over again.'

TEN

Ryker's Ford was full of rumours. The councilmen had spoken to their wives and that had been enough to put the story around town. Ray Bonny still stalked around, perpetually sneering, and in control of a great deal of the finance and employment in the place. He could brazen it out, and nobody dared to make any move against him.

There were plenty who did not want to. They needed him, and they only had contempt for the pot-bellied councilmen who were as crooked as he was but full of pious hypocrisy as they listened to the preacher every Sunday and sang hymns with pompous gusto.

Marshal Warren kept quiet. He spent most of the days at his desk, playing solitaire or sleeping. He kept as far out of sight of the saloon-owner as possible even though he missed the regular payments and free drinks. The mayor fretted as each day passed, but he still hoped that the

Pinkerton Agency would send someone else to take up the case.

But it was not a Pinkerton agent who arrived. Action came from a different source.

It was in the early hours of the morning and Marshal Warren was fast asleep in his narrow bed at the rear of the jailhouse. His room had originally been one of the cells. It had been converted when his wife went back to her folks and he found himself alone in a cabin at the far end of town. It was easier living on the job and not having to go back to a cold, dark place with no stove lit and no coffee on the boil. He was snoring heavily when the persistent tapping began.

The lawman rolled over on his side and listened carefully. It was the back door and the noise seemed to suggest some urgency. He growled miserably and hauled himself out of the cot and onto his sock-covered feet.

'Allright, allright, I'm coming!' he shouted as he lit a candle and crawled into his pants. He staggered out into the passage to open the door with another protest at the noise. His voice was cut short when a large shotgun barrel pushed itself into his unshaven face.

'Just back off gently, Marshal, and don't make no silly moves,' a quiet voice told him. 'You get back there and we'll have no trouble. Just keep goin' to that nice little empty cell at the far end.'

Bert did not pretend to be a hero and backed

along the corridor until he reached the cell that stood with its door invitingly open. He went in without protest, still carrying the candle as he watched another man enter the office. The newcomer lit one of the oil-lamps and came back with the cell-keys from their usual hook behind the marshal's desk. The two men locked him in and looked at each other with quiet satisfaction.

They were young men, dressed like cowpokes but well-armed and with clothes covered in trail dust.

'What the hell do you fellas want?' the marshal asked as he stood the candle on the floor with a spot of hot wax to hold it firmly.

'This ain't anythin' personal, Marshal,' the one with the shotgun told him, 'but we gotta little business in town and we don't figure on havin' a lawman interfere. If you just stay quiet, we'll do what we came to do and be on our way.'

'If you're thinkin' of robbin' the bank, fella. . . !'

'We ain't criminals, Marshal. We're just doin' a little law enforcement ourselves, as you might say. A certain fella that needs a hanging.'

Marshal Warren thought about it for a moment or two.

'You can't be Pinkerton agents. They don't go about lockin' up marshals,' he mused with a certain detachment now that he knew he was safe.

The man grinned to display fine, even teeth.

'No, we ain't. The Pinkerton fellas have done their work and we're finishin' off the job for them.'

'Just the two of you?'

'Hell, no. The rest of the bunch are takin' your Mr Bonny right now.'

And so they were. Five men had broken into the rear door of the Lucky Chance saloon while three others burst in at the front. They all entered the main room, lit only by the pale moonlight, and made for the stairs. As they clattered up to the private quarters of the owner, Ray Bonny appeared on the landing above them. He was partly dressed and carried a shotgun.

The intruders dived for cover as the blasts from the weapon lit up the bar and smashed the walls and front windows of the building. The crashing of glass mingled with the heavy footsteps as the men scrambled up the stairs and tackled the saloon-owner before he could reload. Two of them grappled with him, pushing the man back against the wall as the gun clattered to the floor. There was a shouting that echoed round the high-ceilinged saloon as Ray Bonny was wrestled to the ground and then turned over on his face so that his hands could be tied behind his back. One of the intruders had been wounded and took no part in the skirmish.

They rushed Bonny down the stairs and out of the back door where all their horses were waiting.

The saloon-owner was cursing and shouting for help as lights went on in the town and people began to look through their window-nets at what was happening.

Ray Bonny was bundled onto a horse and the little group set out towards the north. They were soon joined by the two men who had imprisoned the marshal, and the whole bunch moved swiftly over the trail away from Ryker's Ford.

Abel Davis had been wakened by the shotgun blasts but had been unsure of their origin. He got up, lit the oil-lamp, and dressed hurriedly to leave his little cabin and run from the edge of town to the main street. He could see lights in the windows and hear voices in the darkness, but it was several minutes before he reached the jailhouse and found the marshal sitting contentedly in his cell.

The keys had been left on the desk and Abel Davis hurriedly released his boss. The lawman told him what had happened and while Bert Warren went back to his room to dress properly, the deputy left the office to saddle some horses and try to get a few men together to form a posse.

There were plenty of people about now and a few of the younger townsmen were eager to earn the few dollars that they could collect for riding in pursuit of folks who were already far enough away to pose no danger to the pursuers. The men went off to get their horses while Abel and the marshal armed themselves and waited in the main street to be joined by their newly recruited posse.

Somebody had seen the gang galloping off to the north, and that was the direction the marshal took as he led his men in a vain effort to save the saloon-owner. The mayor had been on the scene accompanied by banker Stanley and a few other councilmen. They had shouted encouragement but all stayed behind in the true tradition of political leadership.

The posse rode for about three miles along the worn trail, never quite sure that they were going in the right direction. The marshal hoped that they were not but was tamely following the lead of his deputy who was using the moonlight to keep track of the fleeing gang. The prints of their horses were plain enough in the dry grit on a night of no wind and a low moon that threw sharp shadows.

As they topped a rise, a small grove of trees astride a silvery creek could be seen ahead, and shouts could be heard from the terrified prisoner.

The gang was gathered round a tree that had a low, sweeping branch that overhung the trail. Ray Bonny was struggling on the horse and a rope was being placed round his neck to be thrown over the convenient gallows. It was a lynching.

Abel Davis drew his pistol and fired a warning shot. Some of the other members of the posse did the same thing. The men at the creek turned in alarm before heading off and leaving their prisoner still with the rope dangling from the branch.

They let off a few shots to delay any chase, and one of them fired at Ray Bonny. But their aim was wild and they seemed more intent on putting as much distance as possible between themselves and the revenge of the townsfolk.

The posse galloped down to the creek and surrounded the pale and frightened prisoner. Abel Davis took the noose from around his neck while somebody cut through the cords that held the trembling hands.

'You sure has the luck of the devil,' the marshal said drily as he watched the man rubbing his scarred wrists and trying to recover his dignity.

'And you sure as hell took your time gettin' here,' the saloon-owner snarled. 'I coulda been hanged by that bunch.'

Bert Warren nodded sadly. 'That's certainly the truth,' he admitted, 'but we got here as fast as we could. If you will go around makin' enemies, I figure as how you have to expect a hangin' now and then.'

The posse were grouped around and Ray Bonny looked from one face to another. The creeping daylight showed a lack of sympathy among his rescuers, and he decided to play safe.

'There's five dollars for each of you fellas when we get back home,' he said with an effort to be cheerful. 'And some free drinks at the Lucky Chance.'

That was all it needed to make him feel that he

would be delivered safely to Ryker's Ford, and he was able to relax a little.

'You could still go after that mob,' he suggested to the marshal. 'One of them's nursin' a load of shot from my gun and he won't travel far without a doctor.'

'They're well away by now,' Bert Warren said with conviction. 'We'll just concentrate on gettin' you back to town, so that the folks know you're still in the land of the living.'

The lawman leaned forward in his saddle.

'Who was them fellas, Ray?' he asked in a low voice. 'You must have had some dealin's with them.'

The saloon-owner shook his head in denial.

'That's the hell of it, I don't know,' he insisted. 'They was talkin' about me payin' back for what I did to that Hudson fella. But what in blazes do I know about somethin' that happened twenty years ago?'

'You didn't bushwhack him or do him down on some deal?'

The gaunt man snorted angrily. 'I never even heard tell of him until that Pinkerton business. I thought them agents was after me for other things, but it seems to be somethin' different. Do you know anythin' you ain't been tellin' me?'

'Twenty years ago, Ray, I was out there gettin' my ass shot off by the Yankees.'

The marshal urged his horse forward and led

the posse back the way they had come. Abel Davis rode at his side and leaned over to say a few quiet words.

'Maybe I should follow them fellas,' he suggested. 'If one of them is hurt, he could leave a trail or we could find him dead some place.'

The lawman shrugged. He wanted to get safely back to town.

'Why bother?' he grunted.

'It might help us to know what the hell is goin' on with Bonny. The mayor ain't goin' to be too pleased to find him comin' back alive.'

Bert Warren pondered the idea for a few moments. If he was not accompanied by his deputy when they reached Ryker's Ford, there would be no other lawman to share the credit.

'Yeah, you do that, lad,' he said, 'but don't go bein' no hero. We just need to find out what the hell Bonny and them fellas is all about. It might make things easier with the mayor.'

Abel nodded and swung his horse round to follow the direction the lynch-mob had taken. It was broad daylight now, with a slight wind getting up that would soon wipe out the trail marks.

It took twenty minutes' hard riding before he caught sight of the group ahead of him. They had slowed down, safe in the knowledge that the posse was not on their trail. They were heading due north, crossing a valley ahead of the deputy and making it easy for him to follow without being seen. He was able to track them at a comfortable distance.

There was one puzzling thing. There seemed to be a horse and rider missing from the group. Abel Davis tried to recall how many riders had been gathered round the hanging-tree. He felt that there had been ten, but now he could only count nine men ahead of him.

He soon saw the reason why. As the rising wind blew dust across the trail, the hoof–prints of the animals began to vanish. But there were streaks of blood that seemed to grow larger and then took a sudden turn to the east. He decided to follow this new lead and moved slowly over rocky ground that showed up the blood more clearly while disguising any signs of a horse passing that way. He came to a slight hollow where the soil held enough moisture for some bushes to survive. The horse stood there, looking at him without curiosity as it munched some of the foliage.

A body lay nearby. It was one of the gang; a young man with a damaged leg that had bled from an arterial wound. He was already dead and appeared to have been left by his comrades when they saw that there was nothing they could do for him. He had simply turned off the trail and died.

Abel knelt beside the body and checked for signs of life. It was still warm but a close charge of buckshot from Ray Bonny's gun had done its work effectively. The dead man still wore his .44 Colt and there was a Winchester in the saddle holster of his cow-pony.

The deputy felt in the man's shirt-pockets for some means of identity. There was a vesta-box, a few cents, and a small bag of tobacco. Abel got to his feet and went across to the man's horse. The brand was one he had never seen before; a letter H with a star above it. He took the Winchester from the holster and looked at the stock. The name of Hudson was carved deeply into the wood.

ELEVEN

Things were quiet around Ryker's Ford. The marshal was a hero to many people for having saved the life of one of its prominent citizens. He was not as well-favoured by the mayor who was very disappointed to see Ray Bonny come back alive.

And it was a very scared Ray Bonny. He holed up in his rooms above the saloon and stayed there. The doors had been repaired and strengthened, and the owner carried a gun at his waist as well as the hidden derringer beneath his coat. He shunned all company except for the nightly call from his senior bartenders who brought the takings up to the boss, gave a coded knock, and were then permitted to enter the room.

Abel Davis kept a discreet eye on things. He noted that a bartender had taken a letter to the Wells Fargo office for dispatch on the next stage, and he also noted that lawyer Braddock paid a call on Ray Bonny and was admitted for a conference. Everything was reported to the mayor who waited impatiently for something to happen.

And it did. About three weeks after the lynching attempt. A solitary horseman rode into town and put up at the Ryker House Hotel. He was a tall, thin man of about thirty, with long, dark side-whiskers and a clipped moustache. His eyes were cold and deep-set and he dressed quietly as he moved around town. He talked to nobody and did not seem to have any obvious business to transact.

All that Abel Davis knew was that his name was Ely Jones and that he rode an ex-cavalry mount with an old McClellan saddle. He could once have been a soldier, with his upright bearing and quiet confidence. He spent a lot of time in the Lucky Chance but never appeared the worse for drink.

The mayor was interested in Ely Jones and went into the saloon himself to take a look at the man. He bought a whiskey and stood next to the stranger who was nursing a small glass of cloudy beer as he leaned on the bar.

'I hope they're treatin' you well in our little town,' Steve Ryker said tentatively.

The man turned a cold eye on the little man at his side.

'Well enough,' he answered in a slow, deep voice. 'I'm just passin' through.'

'Indeed? On your way to Mexico?'

'Perhaps.'

'I'm the mayor. Ryker's the name.' He held out a hand and Ely Jones took it limply.

'Howdy, Mr Mayor. You've got a nice town here.'

The voice was almost ironic and Mayor Ryker began to sweat at the effort of getting something out of the man.

'This saloon belongs to a good friend of mine,' he explained to the stranger. 'Ray Bonny's one of our leadin' citizens. Perhaps you've met him?'

'No, can't say I have. He don't seem to be around.'

The mayor sensed that he was being mocked and gave up the struggle. He finished his whiskey, gave the man a nod, and hurriedly left the saloon.

Abel Davis tackled it another way. He went along to the Ryker House Hotel and quietly searched the man's room. There was nothing of real interest there save a good supply of .44 ammunition and a map of the region. He reported to the mayor as ordered and the two just waited for what might happen next. He had already checked the brand on the man's horse, but that told him nothing beyond being a cancelled military mark that seemed to be several years old.

'I don't figure as how he's come to kill Ray Bonny,' the mayor said sadly as he slouched in the chair behind his desk. 'He's been in the Lucky Chance every night since he got here and they seem to accept him. Bonny's got some pretty tough men in that place and in the other saloons. If the fella was dangerous, they'd have set about him before now. Don't you reckon?'

Abel Davis and the marshal were sitting opposite and they both nodded grimly.

'Mr Bonny could be settin' up another gang,' Abel suggested tentatively. 'Maybe goin' back into the hold-up business again.'

The mayor blinked. 'And others could be arrivin' in town to join him?' he asked fearfully. 'And this Jones fella is the first of them?'

'Could be.'

The marshal shifted his large bulk uneasily.

'We could have trouble on our hands,' he murmured.

'You've checked the wanted lists?' the mayor asked.

'Sure have. He ain't on them.'

'I spoke to lawyer Braddock,' the mayor said slowly. 'Now, he's a fella I've known for years, and I reckoned to find out what the hell Bonny wanted with him the other day. But he won't say a word. Just some high-falutin' stuff about client confidentiality. You can never trust them legal fellas, so he won't be gettin' no more business from me. And I told him so.'

Nobody noticed the two men who came into town one evening about a week later. They made their way through the side lanes, riding between rows of corrals before rounding a corner onto the main street where they hitched their mounts outside the Lucky Chance saloon.

There were only a few of the steadier drinkers left there at that time of night. One was sitting on the floor to stop the room going round while another was picking a quarrel with a bartender who was getting ready to settle matters with a pick-axe handle.

All eyes turned on the two men who entered and crossed to the bar. They were young and rough-looking, and both dusty with the weariness of travel stamped on their unshaven faces. They carried guns at their waists and their pale eyes took in the saloon at a glance as they ordered beers. They were served silently and gulped down the welcome liquid.

The quarrelsome drunk left at last and the four poker-players in one corner were getting ready to call it a night. The two strangers looked at each other; the taller one nodded, and they headed for the stairs.

The head bartender shouted a warning but found himself facing a drawn gun. The taller man was striding ahead while the other one covered the rest of the saloon with his pistol. He moved up the stairs walking backwards as he covered his companion from attack by the drinkers. All eyes were turned on them as they headed for the private quarters of Ray Bonny. It was when the first man reached the landing that somebody broke the spell.

A shot rang out that rattled the glasses round

the bar. The man on the landing halted in his stride, looked down at the saloon below, and then raised one hand in what might almost have been a salute before collapsing on the carpet. His companion swung his gun at the man who stood by the bar with a smoking Colt in his right hand.

It was Ely Jones, and a slight grin showed his teeth as he turned the gun on the remaining intruder. They both pulled the triggers at almost the same moment and there was a loud crash of glass as one of the mirrors shattered. Ely Jones still remained facing his opponent who staggered slightly as if trying to climb a few more steps. The man had been shot in the chest but hardly seemed to realize how badly he was hurt. He raised his gun shakily, pulled back the hammer, and tried to aim. Ely fired again. The bullet took the man in almost the same place and he tumbled to his knees before pitching headlong down the stairs. He rolled over at the bottom and then lay still.

Ely Jones put his gun away and signalled to the bartender to fill his glass.

'I guess this one is on the house,' he said in a level voice as he took the drink and raised it to his lips.

The saloon broke into a sudden flood of noise as more people entered and everyone started to talk at once. The doors swung open again to disclose Abel Davis with a shotgun at the ready. The young deputy looked at the two shot men and then glanced round the room to note that the senior bartender was indicating that the man drinking quietly at the bar was the killer.

'What's all this about?' the lawman asked, still holding the shotgun ready for use.

The head bartender explained and Ely Jones listened quietly as his role in the shooting was made clear to the law.

'I thought this was a quiet town,' he said in a dry voice when the tale had been told. 'But a man can't even take a drink in peace.'

Abel Davis bent over the man at the bottom of the stairs. He was quite dead. He went up to look at the fellow on the landing and noticed that despite a wound high in his left side, he was still breathing in a thin and reedy way.

'This one's alive,' the deputy shouted down to the others. 'Go fetch Doc Ferney, Alf.'

One of the poker players left the saloon, anxious to be a part in the drama. He had to push through a crowd that had gathered safely at the windows and in the doorway. Abel looked round at the other occupants of the Lucky Chance.

'Anybody know these fellas?' he asked.

There was a general shaking of heads as the deputy went through the pockets of the two men in an effort to establish an identity. Then he left them and went down the stairs to speak to Ely Jones.

'That was a fancy piece of shootin' you did,

stranger,' he said in a neutral voice. 'Do you know them?'

The man shook his head. 'I was just takin' a quiet drink when they draws guns and heads for the stairs,' he said. 'The barman yells, and I figure as how they're up to no good, so I stops 'em. Seemed the right thing to do at the time.'

'I don't say it weren't. You might also have stopped the owner of this place bein' killed. Do you by any chance know him?'

'Never met the man, and if he's up there, I would have thought all this rumpus would have brought him out to see what was happenin' in his saloon. Don't seem the curious type, do he?'

Abel had to agree, but he knew why Ray Bonny was not showing himself. The man was scared.

Doc Ferney was on the scene in a few minutes, accompanied by the marshal, the mayor, and all the councilmen. The doctor bent over the man and examined the wound with professional relish. His head shook from side to side as he did so, and it was clear from his expression that there was no hope of the man surviving. He looked at the mayor and raised his eyebrows delicately.

'More a case for you than me,' he said cheerfully. 'Real nice bit of shooting.' He looked round at the throng of excited spectators. 'Folk really do seem to have it in for Ray Bonny, don't they?' he murmured.

The man on the floor seemed to have heard the

words and tried to say something. It was a gurgling sound and blood came from his lips in a little stream of frothy bubbles. The doctor bent closer to hear what was being said.

The man muttered something again and Doc Ferney looked up at the mayor.

'He says it ain't nothing personal. Just doing it for the bounty money.'

TWELVE

Mayor Ryker was quite cheerful at the thought that somebody was offering a bounty on Ray Bonny. He sat in the marshal's office with a smile on his face that was very hard to disguise. The lawman was at his desk, Abel Davis stood behind him, and Ely Jones occupied a chair opposite the three men.

'Now, I ain't sayin' as how you've done anythin' wrong,' the marshal said in his official voice, 'but you is a stranger in town and them two fellas back there was bounty hunters. You could be one as well. How in hell do we know you ain't gonna claim Roy Bonny for yourself?'

The man grinned slightly and shifted his bulk in the chair.

'If I was gonna kill this fella Bonny,' he said, 'I'd have done it and been on my way to claim the bounty right now. All that happened is that I was havin' a drink and them folks started trouble. I just acted like any law-abidin' fella would. You got any complaint about that, Marshal?'

There was a certain edge to the last words and Bert Warren hastened to assure him that he had not.

'I think that all the marshal wants to know,' the mayor asked quietly, 'is why our little town is favoured by your presence?'

The stranger's cold eyes rested on the mayor's portly figure with an almost contemptuous glance.

'I like your town,' he said. 'But I also got business here. Private family business.'

He reached under his dark shirt and removed a small chamois bag. The others watched eagerly as the man turned out the contents on to the desk top. There were a few gold coins which rolled around for a moment, but it was the wad of banknotes that made their mouths drop open. The mayor leaned forward and poked at the pile of money.

'There must be three or four hundred dollars there,' he said with the respect due to wealth.

'Somethin' like that. I ain't a poor man, and I ain't no ten-cent bounty hunter. I got family business in the neighbourhood and I don't mean to harm no one who don't harm me.'

The man rose from the chair, picked up the money and put it away again.

'And now I'll be off to my bed,' he said as he headed for the door.

They watched him go and then all three looked at each other as if for inspiration.

'If he ain't a bounty hunter,' the mayor said thoughtfully, 'he could be here to protect Ray Bonny. And that's a damned sight worse. He's too good with a gun.'

'It's a pity that fella didn't live long enough to tell us why the bounty was bein' offered,' the marshal said bitterly. 'Somebody certainly has it in for our saloon boss. And I'd sure as hell like to know who.'

'And why,' the mayor added.

'Has Mr Bonny showed himself yet?' Abel Davis asked. 'There's been enough upset tonight to bring the whole town outa bed.'

The mayor nodded. 'Doc Ferney knocked on his door and had a talk with him. The man's scared to hell and ain't comin' outa hidin' until he knows it's safe. I can tell you one thing for sure. He ain't plannin' on makin' no more raids against the stage line.'

'Maybe he'll leave town now,' the marshal suggested hopefully.

The mayor shook his head. 'Not without half the Yankee army to guard his ass, he won't. I figure as how we're stuck with him until another bounty hunter comes to town. And don't you two get quick on the trigger until it's all over. We need Ray Bonny dead or runnin' like hell for Mexico.'

The mayor was to be disappointed if he thought the saloon-owner was going to head south, but the man still kept out of sight while a couple of weeks passed with nothing to disturb the dull routine of Ryker's Ford.

Ely Jones was in the Lucky Chance one evening, having a drink, when Abel Davis walked in. The two men nodded to each other but stayed apart as they drank the warm beer. The place was not very busy so early in the week and only two bartenders were on duty.

The deputy was almost on the point of leaving when the doors swung open and three men entered. They were not noisy or disorderly in any way but just went quietly to the bar and bought drinks like ordinary cowpokes. They stood together and chatted quietly and did not seem to be a possible source of any trouble.

All were young, armed with Colt .44 pistols, and looked as if they had travelled some distance. The head bartender appeared to accept them happily, and after a few minutes, Abel Davis noticed that he disappeared up the stairs to have a word with his boss.

To the surprise of all the regular customers, Ray Bonny came down a few minutes later. He was freshly shaven, neatly dressed, and walked with his usual air of arrogant contempt for the world. He crossed to an empty table and the three young men joined him. Abel Davis was pretty sure that they were the answer to the letter that had worried the mayor.

118

He looked along the bar to where Ely Jones stood watching the arrival of the owner. The man seemed interested but there was a look on his face that was hard to interpret. The deputy moved along the counter until he was next to the man.

'That's our Mr Bonny,' he said quietly. 'Come out of hidin' to greet a few friends.'

Ely Jones looked at the lawman for a moment as if considering something.

'How do you get on with Bonny?' he asked.

'I don't. He's back of a lotta hold-ups, but somebody else always takes the bullet. I'd like to see him behind bars – or hanged. And you?'

The man took a sip of his beer and pulled a face at the taste of the stuff.

'Is your marshal of the same mind?' he asked.

'He's on the side the mayor tells him to be on. They're kin.'

Ely Jones nodded as if agreeing with himself.

'I figured some sort of set-up like that in a small town like Ryker's Ford. All the important folk kin to one another and goin' back a lotta years. Is Bonny any kin to them?'

'No, he's an incomer. They tell me he's been here about twenty years and he's not exactly the friendly sort. I reckon you've got an interest in Ray Bonny. Maybe you and me are on the same side.'

'Could be.' The man called to the bartender to order some more drinks. 'Maybe we should sit

119

ourselves down somewheres a bit private and have a little talk.'

They took their glasses to an empty table in the far corner and settled down opposite each other.

'Twenty years ago,' Ely Jones said quietly, 'a fella who was kin to me died somewheres not too far from Ryker's Ford.'

'By the name of Hudson?'

Ely Jones blinked and then gave a slight grin.

'Well, ain't you a know-all son-of-a-bitch deputy,' he said softly. 'That's a fact. I'm Will Hudson and Jack Hudson was my pa.'

'And you're after the man who killed him.' Abel Davis said.

It was a statement rather than a question and the newly named Will Hudson nodded soberly.

'Wouldn't you be?' he asked.

'I sure as hell would, and the law ain't got no kick comin' if it's a clean fight and no shootin' in the back, sort of thing. You reckon that Ray Bonny is the man?'

'I figure so. I'd better tell you what it's all about. But first, how did you know it were my pa?'

Abel Davis told him about the hat being found twenty years ago and the man listened patiently as the meagre story unfolded.

'Well, that makes sense now,' he said when it was over. 'You see, the war was comin' to an end, and my pa was in one hell of a bind. He'd been supplyin' the Confederacy with meat and horses.

Got paid in Southern money, and that seemed fine. Then it all went sour when the Yankees drove back our army and my pa's spread was on the point of endin' up in Yankee hands.'

He shook his head sadly. 'I were only ten years old at the time but I can still remember the talk round the table at night. Ma and Pa could lose everythin' if the Confederate money suddenly became worthless. And it was sure headin' that way. So Pa decided to do somethin' about it. He and my elder brother went south with all our family's money to exchange it for Mexican silver pesos. One or two other families had done it, and although it don't seem very loyal, it sure as hell meant the difference between survival and ruin for us.'

He shook his head again. 'And that was the last we heard of them. They just never came back.'

He paused for a few moments and took a long drink of the warm beer.

'We was nigh on ruined anyways,' he went on. 'The Yankees took our cattle and horses, burned down the house, and left us with nothin' but a few hogs and a lotta problems. Ma brought me up with a little help from her family and the neighbours, and eventually things got back to normal. But we never knew what happened to Pa and my elder brother. Just reckoned that they'd run into a Yankee patrol or met up with bushwhackers. Then Ma went visitin' some relatives down in Tombstone about twelve months ago. And she sees this newspaper office with a photograph in the window about some election in a town called Ryker's Ford.'

He pointed to the framed copy that adorned the far wall.

'That's the one,' he said, 'and it showed all your local councilmen decked out in their go-to-meetin' best. One of them is wearin' my pa's watch chain. That gold-nugget ain't easy to miss and we'd all know its shape anywhere. Ma remembered that Pa intended to cross the river on a ferry at a place called Ryker's Ford. It was high-water season and it was the best crossin'-point to Mexico.'

'So you employed the Pinkerton people to make enquiries?' Abel Davis suggested.

'That's right. We live one hell of a way from here, and I'm busy runnin' the ranch. So Ma contacted these fellas and they started costin' us money like it was fresh molasses. We're told that one got himself killed and another has disappeared. But that last fella identified Ray Bonny as bein' the man with the watch-chain and still livin' in your town. We couldn't afford no more hired help, so Ma offered some of the local lads a bounty if they could get him. They ain't done nothin' I hear tell of, so I had to come myself.'

Abel Davis told him exactly what the bounty hunters had done and how they had ended up. The man with the marked Winchester had been a Hudson ranch hand, and all the others were

122

cowpokes trying to make a few dollars in the off-season.

'And now he seems to be gettin' a new gang together,' Will Hudson said bitterly as he watched Ray Bonny ordering more drinks for the three men at his table.

'Yeah, and unless they make trouble in town, there ain't a thing the law can do about it,' Abel said with equal bitterness. 'Do you aim to take him on?'

'I have to. Last of the line, you might say. There's only Ma and me, though I aims to get myself married when I've settled this business.'

Abel looked across the room.

'If you tangle with that lot, I don't reckon your marryin' chances as bein' too good. What's your next move?'

'I thought I saw a gun under his coat when he came down them stairs.'

'You did, and he always carries a derringer. If them three fellas were to leave, you'd be able to call him out fair and square. There are enough folk here to bear witness to a shoot-out, and I reckon as how the law wouldn't be interested. And the mayor would be almighty pleased.'

Will smiled slightly. 'So I have to hope them three fellas leave before he goes scuttlin' back upstairs?'

'Maybe not. Their horses are outside at the rail. They might just break loose, get spooked, and go careerin' down the street. These things happen. I figure as how the owners would go chasin' after them, don't you?'

Will Hudson did not answer as he studied the face of the lawman. He just nodded silently when Abel stood up to leave.

'I gotta be gettin' off home now,' the deputy said quietly. 'I gotta long day tomorrow.'

When the doors had swung closed again behind the deputy, Will Hudson went back to the bar. He moved to a position only a few feet away from the group at the table and where he could step between Ray Bonny and the stairs. He waited for something to happen.

It soon did. There was a burst of shouting outside the saloon and the sound of horses neighing and galloping. Some of the Lucky Chance drinkers went to the windows and looked out at the commotion.

'The hitchin'-rail's broke!' one of them shouted as he ran for the door. 'The horses is all loose and spooked to hell and back.'

The three men who'd been sitting with Ray Bonny rushed after the man to get their own mounts. There was a sudden lull in the saloon as only the few drinkers not using horses were left to watch the fun or finish their beers.

Ray Bonny was also left, and stood for a moment, not quite realizing that his protection had vanished and that he was alone. He turned for the staircase and found a stranger standing in front of him, a few steps above, and blocking the way.

Will Hudson held up a restraining hand to the saloon-owner.

'I've been waitin' for you, Bonny,' he said tersely. 'You murdered my kin and now it's my turn to kill you. Draw.'

The gaunt man went even more pale as he stood at the foot of the stairs. His lips were dry but he tried to talk calmly.

'Look, fella,' he grated, 'I don't go around shootin' folks and I don't know who the hell you are. I just run a few saloons. Ask anybody round here.'

He glanced eagerly round the room, hoping that one of his customers would speak up for him or that he could play for enough time. The place was silent as everybody watched the two men facing each other.

'Don't the name Hudson mean anythin' to you anymore?' the stranger asked.

'I keep hearin' it, but it don't make no sense. I never knew anybody named Hudson. What the hell is this all about?'

'My pa and my brother were in this part of the world about twenty years ago. They was bush-whacked, and you got some of the loot right there on your fancy waistcoat. Now draw.'

Will Hudson's right hand went down towards his

holster and Ray Bonny knew that there was no time left. He dropped his own hand and the two guns sprang out at almost the same time. The deafening noise of the shots echoed round the saloon and the drinkers watched the owner stagger back against the wall. He tried to raise the pistol again, and then collapsed on the sawdusted floor.

They turned their eyes on the younger man who stood on the staircase. There was a smile on his face at a job well done, and then the smile vanished as he fell against the rail and tumbled to the bottom of the stairs. Both men were dead.

THIRTEEN

It was many years since Mayor Ryker had enjoyed a funeral so much. That of his rich mother-in-law had brought a smile to his face, but such occasions were few and far between. He lit a cigar as he strolled from the burial ground in company with the other town dignitaries.

Burying Ray Bonny had brought out the crowds. People flocked to the lavish funeral that the mayor had laid on. He was safe in the knowledge that there was plenty of money to pay for it. The funeral of Will Hudson had been more modest. All the man had of value would be going back to a widowed mother up north.

The mayor led the way to the mortician's building where there were a few bottles of good whiskey to be consumed while important affairs were discussed. Banker Stanley sweated at his side, the lanky lawyer Braddock walked sedately a little behind them, and Marshal Warren ambled along in his usual manner. Abel Davis watched them enter the funeral parlour before going his own way to the jailhouse where he would read or play solitaire.

The mayor seated his friends round a table and poured drinks. The fact that Will Hudson's body had lain on the table a few hours back did not put the councilmen off their liquor. As they were raising glasses to a mutual toast, Judge Mason came hurrying in, wheezing as usual as he thrust his skinny frame into an empty chair. He took a glass of whiskey thankfully.

'I think we've just done a good day's work, gentlemen,' the mayor said as he drank. 'Ray Bonny sure as hell gave this town a bad name. If it ever got out that he was behind all them stage robberies, we'd never live it down. Folks would be askin' why we didn't put an end to him sooner.'

They all cast sly glances at the marshal but he pretended not to notice.

'Well, now we got a serious matter to work out,' Mayor Ryker went on. 'Ray Bonny's got folks workin' for him, and there's property to be looked after. And since he ain't got no kin. . . .'

Lawyer Braddock eased his long body to a more comfortable position and coughed to attract attention.

'That ain't so,' he said heavily. 'Ray Bonny's got a widowed sister, and she has two sons.'

There was a dead silence in the room as they all looked at the lawyer and hoped that he was making the first joke in his life.

'That can't be,' the mayor croaked. 'We never heard tell of no kin in twenty years or more.'

'Well, you're hearing it now. He came to me a short time back and made a will. The fella was scared to hell with all them Pinkerton people on his tail. So I drew it up and everything he has in Ryker's Ford goes to his sister and two nephews.'

The mayor, the judge, and the marshal just looked at each other while the banker sat passively. It did not matter to him. Whoever inherited, there was only one bank in town.

'But that's . . .' The mayor tried not to look too disappointed. 'That's most unexpected,' he managed to say. 'Are these kin of his goin' to sell the businesses or try runnin' them like he did?'

The lawyer shrugged his high shoulders.

'Ray Bonny left a letter for them to pick up when they arrive in town. He reckons it will tell them how he's got things fixed up here.' He looked round the table. 'And who he's got on his payroll,' he added drily.

The meeting broke up a short time later. Only the lawyer and the banker seemed happy at the outcome. Marshal Warren stayed behind with the mayor and the judge while Len Stanley stopped in at the jailhouse where Abel Davis was making himself a cup of coffee. He poured out one for the moneylender and the two men sat opposite each other across the old desk.

'There are a few things about this business that I don't rightly understand, Abel,' the banker said as he sipped the hot drink. 'Suppose you tell me why this fella Hudson wanted to kill Ray Bonny. Was it somethin' to do with one of them stage hold-ups that I'm told he organized?'

Abel shook his head. 'Seems to be a different sorta killin' spree,' he said slowly. 'As I figured it from what Will Hudson told me, it was because his pa was carryin' money and Ray Bonny just bushwhacked him for it. Took the money and that watch-chain he wore.'

He explained how the Hudson family had recognized the nugget from a newspaper photograph and how things had developed from that moment. Banker Stanley had listened silently, but at a mention of the gold-nugget, his head went up as if he had been bitten by a hornet.

'But that can't be so,' he said forcibly. 'That just can't be so.'

'How do you reckon that, Mr Stanley?' Abel asked.

'Ray Bonny never stole that chain and nugget. He bought them fair and square. Came to me at the bank to withdraw the cash money, he did. I recall it as plain as if it happened yesterday. You got the story all wrong, fella.'

'You'd better tell me what happened, Mr Stanley.' Abel's voice was low and anxious.

'Well, Ray Bonny came to town and deposited

money at my bank. We'd only just opened for business and he was one of the first big customers. I was real impressed and curious to know what his profession was. He wouldn't say but I sorta took it for granted that he was a cattle-trader. That was how money was made in those days. Horses and beef for the Confederate army. Then he started buying into local saloons or opening new ones. He grew into a really big man, and I reckon we all treated him carefully.'

The banker wiped sweat from his forehead with a large yellow bandanna which he then thrust back into his coat-pocket.

'I remember the business about the Hudson hat. There weren't anything to it at the time. Just a hat and no head to fit it. There were never any enquiries and I figure that none of us thought of it again. Bonny came to town several months after that find, and it was maybe a couple of months after arriving that he came into the bank one day with a fellow who lived up Santa Rosa way. He drew some money from his account and handed it over to this fella. Right there in the bank. Then the fella gave him a watch and chain. And that fancy nugget was part of the deal. Ray Bonny bought it there and then, straight in front of my eyes. I reckoned that him and the seller didn't trust each other unless there were witnesses.'

'And who was the fella?' Abel Davis asked tensely.

'Name of Sam Cole. He has a small place just outside Santa Rosa. Must be getting on for sixty now, I reckon. I don't know where the hell he got something of that value, but it could be that he was the one who bushwhacked Hudson.'

'Could be. Did Sam Cole sell anythin' else in town about that time?'

Banker Stanley thought hard for a moment.

'I never knew much about him,' he said slowly. 'He weren't the sort to have anything to do with banks. I vaguely recall that he sold some saddlery at about that time and he was offering two Colt Navy pistols around. We didn't have a gun-store in those days and they were a popular type of weapon. More to be found in the north than down here. He must have sold them because he spent a few days getting drunk and then headed outa town when his wife showed up and lambasted him something awful. It was quite a scene and that woman could sure use language. That's what makes it stick in my mind.' The moneylender chuckled at the memory.

'Does he come into town these days?' Abel asked.

'I don't rightly know. I certainly ain't seen him for a few years. Could be dead. Or hanged.'

'Why hanged, Mr Stanley?'

The banker squinted at the deputy through piggy little eyes.

'That spread of his wouldn't support a family of

132

gophers. I always reckoned him for some sort of rustler. Or worse. I figure that if you're looking for the killer of the Hudson fella, look around Santa Rosa way.'

'I might just do that.'

The banker gave the young man a shrewd glance.

'Outside your territory, ain't it? They got a marshal there.'

'You might say it's personal,' the deputy said quietly. 'I think I owe it to Will Hudson. Maybe even to Ray Bonny.'

'And will Marshal Warren go along with that?'

'No, but then I ain't gonna tell him. Are you?'

The banker smiled. 'I ain't gonna tell him either. Your boss man ain't the sort of marshal we need in a decent town. If it weren't for him being the mayor's kin, he'd be hard pushed to clean up after the horses in a livery stable. I didn't like Ray Bonny, but he was a good customer of the bank and he gave a lotta folks work in these parts. Maybe you have a sense of justice, young fella. Good luck to you.'

Abel Davis only had a vague idea about the location of the Cole farm. He had been told that it lay in a valley by a small creek and was exactly ten miles south of Santa Rosa. He travelled for two days towards the spot, accompanied by a mule to carry his gear and safe in the knowledge that Bert

Warren was not going to need him.

The Ryker's Ford marshal could relax now that the three men visiting the late saloon-owner had departed as soon as they saw his dead body. He did not need his deputy in a town as quiet as Ryker's Ford now was, and was glad not to have to share the office space.

Abel's story of tracking down a report of some rustling was as good as any and Marshal Warren could sleep at his desk.

The young deputy reached the area on the third day. There was some worn fencing and a collection of hogs which shared the land with poultry. A small cabin occupied some high ground and there was smoke coming from the iron stovepipe. He could see no other sign of life and decided to approach carefully.

He withdrew from sight of the cabin and rode quietly round the perimeter of the wire to a dip in the ground behind the creek. There were a few horses and a couple of mules in the better pasture down there and he suddenly smelled something that was hauntingly familiar. Burning hair.

Somebody was branding cattle. It was a smell that he had known since his childhood on a ranch in northern Texas. The young deputy reined in his horse and listened. Over the ridge ahead of him there was a faint hint of smoke and he could just catch voices and the lowing of the restless steers.

He dismounted and looked around for a clump

of bushes to which he could tie his animals. They could not be trusted by just letting the reins trail on the ground. He found a low bramble that sheltered a few lizards and tethered them there. Then he moved forward slowly towards the spot where the voices could be heard.

There were two young fellows in the dip below. They had a fire going and branding-irons were heating up in it. About thirty steers were penned into an old corral which was held together with rusty wire and bits of tree-branches. There were no calves among them and it was obvious that old brands were being changed on fully grown animals.

It meant only one thing. Rustlers. Abel Davis felt better at the sight of them as he loosened the pistol at his belt. He decided to go back for his shotgun and edged away again to get the weapon from the saddle holster.

With the shotgun held in the crook of his arm, he walked down the slope and confronted the two men as they got ready to brand a steer. One was holding the animal's head firmly and the other was readying the branding iron. The steer was too old to be wrestled to the ground and a firm grip had been used on the halter round its head. Abel noted that they both carried guns at their belts and that a shotgun lay against a wooden pail a short distance away.

As he topped the rise and stood above them,

they both reacted by jumping backwards and swinging in the deputy's direction. The one with the iron let it fall on the grass and went for his gun. The other man released the headband on the steer and had to jump clear as it kicked its way to freedom.

'Hold it there, fellas,' Abel called as he pointed the gun with the hammers back on both barrels. 'Just don't do nothin' hasty and I won't be spoilin' your weddin' chances.'

The two young men saw the steadily held weapon and noted the badge on Abel's waistcoat. They looked at each other and seemed to decide not to tangle with an experienced gun-handler.

'We ain't doin' nothin' wrong,' one of them ventured. 'These is our pa's cattle.'

'Is that a fact now?' Abel grinned. 'And he's changin' his brand this year? Well, these things happen, I guess. Now, would your pa be Sam Cole?'

They nodded dumbly and the deputy noticed that they were gradually edging away from each other. He knew the old trick and decided that the one who had held the branding-iron was likely to draw first. He looked to be the brains of the family with a thin face and sly eyes that glanced nervously from side to side.

'I just want a word with your pa,' Abel said slowly, 'and I don't want you fellas gettin' any wrong ideas. I ain't here to arrest folks for cattle-stealin' and suchlike. I just want to ask a few questions about somethin' that happened a lotta years back. So let's not get excited. Where is your pa? The chimney's smokin' back there, so don't try lyin' to me.'

The two looked at each other and the sly one answered.

'Yeah, he's back at the cabin, Marshal,' he said slowly, 'but he ain't a well man. Don't get around these days, and he ain't done nothin' against the law. Ain't even left the spread for a year or so.'

'Glad to hear it. Let's go see him. You fellas just drop them belts and then walk in front of me.'

The two men started to do what they were told. They were some yards apart now and Abel kept the shotgun trained on the sly one. He watched as their hands went down to the buckles of the gunbelts and they began to unfasten them.

The move came from the other brother. It took the deputy by surprise when the young fellow unfastened the belt but caught the falling gun with a dazzling speed. He had it from the holster and cocked before Abel could properly react.

The deputy swung round clumsily and pulled the trigger of the right-hand barrel. The shotgun went off with a recoil that hurt his unprepared arm. The charge took the young man full in the chest and he seemed almost to leap backwards before falling in a pile of shattered bone and blood.

The other brother drew his own gun as the belt slipped to the ground. But he did not fire. The sight of the dead man was enough to make him drop the weapon and he stood helplessly in front of the deputy.

'You killed Ned!' he cried in a choked voice. 'You killed him!'

'You're smart. Now let's go see your pa.'

The young man looked numb as he led the way over the slope towards the cabin where a man was at the door with a shotgun in his hands. He saw the two men approach and looked uncertainly at the badge the deputy wore.

'We don't want any more shooting!' Abel shouted as they got nearer. 'Just drop that gun and come out to where we can talk.'

Sam Cole looked at his remaining son and seemed to know that his other boy was dead. He lowered the gun gently and placed it against the cabin wall. Then he walked slowly to where a horse-trough stood, part-filled with stagnant fluid around which gnats happily buzzed. He sat down on the edge of it, a weary and sick man with a thin, drawn face and stooped shoulders.

'It was only a few head of steers,' he said in a husky voice. 'Not worth killin' over, Marshal.'

Abel motioned the young man to go sit next to his father. He stood in front of them and had a moment of regret over the killing. But it had been a near thing and he could have been lying back there instead of young Cole. He cleared his throat and put on an official air.

'This ain't about cattle,' he said firmly. 'It's about somethin' that happened back in Ryker's Ford some twenty years ago. You sold Ray Bonny a watch and chain. Do you recall the deal?'

The elderly man looked puzzled for a moment and then his pale eyes widened a little.

'Sure,' he murmured. 'That were in the last days of the war. Come to think of it, it had just ended, and that Bonny fella paid me in Yankee dollars. Yeah, I recall it now. But what the hell does it matter after all this time?'

'Where did you get the watch?'

There was a long silence and then the old man gave vent to a crackling noise deep in his throat which, Abel Davis realized, was an attempt at a chuckle.

'Well, if you're figurin' on arrestin' me for that, Marshal,' the man wheezed, 'you sure as hell is too late. I ain't got long enough to go to court and be mixed up with all them legal fellas.'

'Just tell me all about it,' Abel said patiently.

'I didn't kill nobody for that gold watch,' Sam Cole said self-righteously. 'It were just there for the takin' as you might say.'

He sniffed and felt in his pocket for a little plug of chewing tobacco. He bit off a piece and offered the rest to the deputy. Abel shook his head and the old man returned it to his pocket.

'It was in the last months of the war,' the man said slowly as he chewed. 'Me and Billy Griffiths were movin' a few cattle around to fresh pasture, as you might say. We decided to stay the night by a creek just north of Ryker's Ford. Then we aimed to cross into Mexico the next day. The animals smelt the water and went ahead of us, and when we got there, the first thing we spotted was a couple of horses.'

He spat out a stream of juice and wiped his mouth.

'And then we saw the bodies. Two fellas, they was. A young one shot in the back, and the older one lyin' in the middle of a dyin' fire. He was shot in the chest. The young fella had been sleepin' when it happened. He was still wrapped in blankets. It was as sure as hell a bushwhackin' affair. Funny thing was, nothin' was stole from them that I could see. They had their guns and saddles, and there was even some money in their pokes. Twenty dollars or more. It was the weirdest thing I ever did come across.'

'So you took everythin' you saw?'

The old man grinned. 'We sure as hell did, Marshal. Lookit, we was dirt poor, and here was horses, saddles, and guns. And then I spotted the watch, and that was what caused the trouble. Billy wanted it real bad. He'd never owned one and I already had a little pinchbeck thing. He thought he should have it and I reckon we had a fallin' out.

He got hisself killed and I was left with the lot.'

He licked his lips at the memory.

'They was sure sweet pickings, Marshal. I had one hell of a job managin' without Billy, but I hid the saddles and guns near the creek, took the cattle and horses over the border to sell, and then came back for the rest of the stuff. I sold most of it at Ryker's Ford a few months later. Ray Bonny took a fancy to that nugget on the watch-chain and he paid a good price.'

There was a long silence while the gnats grew bolder and flew into the faces of the three men who disturbed their occupation of the stagnant horse-trough.

'Do you think I killed them fellas?' Sam Cole suddenly asked.

'I don't know. Did you?'

'Well, it is confessin' time, and I owned to stealin' cattle, and pickin' up the watch and a few other things, but I ain't a killer. Never killed a fella but in a fair shoot-out. That's the honest-to-God truth, Marshal.'

'I like your story, Sam,' the deputy said slowly, 'and I ain't aimin' to make trouble over a few head of cattle. I'm concerned about the man who owned that watch. Nothin' more. Have you told me everythin' about that day?'

There was another long pause and then the old man took a deep and painful breath.

'Marshal,' he said slowly, 'me and my boy here

got about fifty cents between us. Now, that's rock-bottom poor. A fella has his little secrets, and a fella has his needs. If you've got a few dollars in your poke, maybe me and you could do a deal.'

FOURTEEN

Abel Davis was thoughtful as he rode back to Ryker's Ford. What he had been told might be true, or it might be just a story made up by a man who wanted to wheedle a few dollars out of someone gullible enough to part with money. The young deputy had given old Sam Cole all the spare cash he was carrying. It totalled three dollars and a few cents. If the information was true, it was a good investment, but needed careful consideration.

He entered town in the early evening, timing his arrival so that he would meet nobody in authority who might ask questions as to where he had been for several days. After washing and taking a meal, he called on the banker and found the stout man sweating away as usual in the comfort of his own home where Mrs Stanley was sewing under the bright lamplight, and two noisy little girls were playing with dolls and a string-puppet.

Abel apologized for intruding so late but explained that he had only just got back to town

143

after seeing the man mentioned by the banker.

'So old Sam is still alive then,' the moneylender mused. 'Still leading a pure life?'

The deputy grinned. 'As pure as rustlin' cattle can make it,' he said. 'But he ain't got much longer to go, I reckon. He's a mighty sick man.'

'It's all that chewing of tobacco that causes it,' Len Stanley said wisely. 'I suppose he still does it?'

Abel nodded.

'Well, that's his trouble. Any doctor will tell you that tobacco ain't for chewing. It's for smoking in a civilized manner. So, did he kill Jack Hudson?'

'He reckons not. All this happened so long ago that I was only a kid, bare able to understand all about the war. Tell me, Mr Stanley, what would a man do if he wanted to change his Confederate money into somethin' safer? How would he go about it?'

'Well now, that is a big question.' The banker nestled back in his chair while Mrs Stanley listened to what was being said with open curiosity. 'Fellas like that were in a real bind. If they tried changing for Yankee dollars and folks heard about it, they could find themselves run out of town or even tarred and feathered. So they slipped across the border into Mexico. You see, at that time, the Mexicans were having their own troubles. The French had given them an emperor, there'd been a civil war, and nothing was very stable.

'But Mexicans didn't know how weak the

Confederate money was. So they would sell silver pesos and French Louis d'or coins for our dollars. There was also silver jewellery. The Mexicans specialized in that, I had quite a few ranchers would leave little boxes of gold and silver gewgaws at the bank for safety as they travelled around. Then there were the fellas who sold horses and cattle across the border instead of supplying the Confederate army. They collected in safe money instead of our increasingly worthless stuff. Folk were playing cautious whenever the chance arose. You can't really blame them.'

'I guess not. I think you said that Ray Bonny had Yankee dollars when he came to town. Am I right?'

'That's correct. Yankee dollars.' The banker seemed a bit surprised at his own memory. 'I hadn't thought about it before, but he had all Yankee dollars. They was legal at that stage and he wasn't a local so nobody would have thought about him being disloyal to the South. Why do you ask, lad?'

Abel Davis thought about it for a moment or two.

'I got somethin' naggin' at me,' he admitted. 'Suppose you wanted to bushwhack a fella for his money. Would you bother about him carryin' Confederate notes, or would you wait until he'd been across the border and was bringin' back somethin' else in the way of cash?'

The banker laughed until his fat frame shook.

'That's easy, lad. Get him on the way back. Good solid silver or gold that wouldn't lose its value.'

'So did any of our local citizens suddenly have a lot of silver or gold Mexican money around that time?'

The banker's face went blank for a moment and there was a long, awkward silence.

'Well, now you are getting into deep water, lad,' the moneylender said quietly. 'I can't be telling tales, and I might be accusing the wrong folks. You'd better tread warily. Like I do.'

'Oh, I mean to do just that, Mr Stanley. That's why I'm gettin' all the facts before I go reportin' to the mayor or the marshal. I don't want to cause trouble for nobody who ain't guilty. Tell me, who's taken over the stuff that belonged to Will Hudson? He had a good horse and plenty of cash money on him.'

The banker seemed a bit relieved at the turn of the conversation.

'Lawyer Braddock,' he said. 'He was quick to grab the business, and they tell me he's in touch with the young fellow's family up north. Why do you ask?'

'I need a word with lawyer Braddock, if he's at home.'

'Oh, he'll be at home tonight. He don't go to the saloon and there's no hymn-singing in the middle of the week.'

Abel Davis bade the banker a good night and

went down the street to where the town lawyer lived in a plain house which had a neatness and coldness about it to match the owner's character. The deputy was admitted by the sour-faced man and taken into a cold room which smelt vaguely damp. Mrs Braddock could be heard pottering about in the kitchen.

'I'm sorry to trouble you, Mr Braddock,' the lawman said, 'but I need to know if any of Will Hudson's kin are comin' to town to deal with his affairs.'

'I'm informed that there will be such a visit,' the lawyer replied in his grating voice. 'I have been in touch with the family and expect somebody in the near future. Is this of importance?'

'It may be. You see, there is a chance that Ray Bonny did not kill Will Hudson's father. If that's the case, another member of the Hudson family could come lookin' for the real killer.'

The lawyer's eyes narrowed as he considered the matter.

'That poses some interesting problems,' he murmured. 'And if there are doubts of Bonny's guilt, then perhaps another name is being suggested.'

He looked hard at the deputy and Abel sensed that Mrs Braddock was somewhere close by, listening to every word.

'I can't tell you what banker Stanley and I talked about,' Abel said carefully, 'but it don't appear that

Ray Bonny committed that particular hold-up.'

Mr and Mrs Braddock were discussing the matter almost before the deputy was out of the door. And Abel Davis knew that Mrs Braddock was a close friend of Len Stanley's wife. He went to bed with the knowledge that he had done a good day's work. There would be a lot of gossip around town tomorrow.

He reported to the marshal early the next morning, telling a tale of tracking rustlers but never quite catching up with them. The lawman was not very interested. He was too preoccupied with how he could ingratiate himself with the new owner of the three saloons in order to obtain some sort of weekly pay-off.

The mayor took quite a different attitude. He sat behind his desk in the cramped little office and glared at the newly returned deputy.

'Where the hell have you been?' he asked angrily. 'My housekeeper told me this morning that she heard some damn-fool story about Ray Bonny not bushwhackin' the Hudson fella. Have you heard tell of this?'

'That's what I've been checkin' on, Mr Mayor,' Abel answered calmly as he took an uninvited seat. 'I been out to have a word with the fella who might have done it.'

The mayor looked interested now and his anger subsided.

'Is that a fact? And who would that be?' he asked.

'Old Sam Cole. He was the one Ray Bonny got the watch and nugget from. Cole also sold off Hudson's horses, saddles, and guns.'

Mayor Ryker's chubby face broke into a smile.

'Well, that was a good job you did, fella. You'll go far in this town. Have you brought him in?'

'No, he's a sick man, and I don't reckon to him killin' Hudson and his son. Somebody else did that, and stole all the silver pesos Hudson was carryin' back from Mexico.'

'Is that a fact now? So what do you figure happened out there all them years ago?'

Abel leaned back in the bentwood chair.

'Well now, I reckon as how Jack Hudson and his son came south and passed through Ryker's Ford, It was the time of year when the water in the river was high, so they'd cross on your pa's ferry. They was carryin' Confederate money at the time, but when they returned, they'd be carryin' Mexican pesos. They went through Ryker's Ford again and stopped for the night at the creek. Some fella followed them from here, killed them both, and started searchin' for that load of silver. He probably meant to take the horses and everythin' else as well, but things went awful wrong.'

Abel Davis stopped talking and licked his dry lips. He could have used a drink but the mayor was not breaking out any whiskey today.

'Go on,' the First Citizen prompted impatiently.

'Well, just as he was gettin' ready to take the rest

of their belongin's, some cattle came on the scene. They had smelt the water and it was a mighty pleasin' thing to come across after a long day on the trail. The killer knew he had to skip out because the cowpokes would be close behind. And so they was. And one of them recognized the killer as he took off like a scared jackrabbit, headin' back for town.'

There was a long silence and Abel could smell the other man's sweat as well as see the lines of it trailing down his face.

'And Sam Cole told you all this?' the mayor asked in a low voice.

'Eventually.'

'And you believed him?'

'Only when I asked a question back here in town. I needed to know who paid silver pesos into the bank at that time.'

'Stanley had no right. . . !'

'He didn't talk, but his face gave it away. And his wife was listenin' to every word.'

'My God!'

The mayor's hands were trembling on the desk top.

'I didn't want to do it, Abel,' he said. 'My pa was a hard man. This town was built round the ferry, and he ruled everybody like some sorta slave-owner. He guessed what Hudson and his son was doin' when they crossed into Mexico. And when they came back, he sent me to get the money off them. I'm no gun-totin' fella. I couldn't just hold up two men, take their money and then hope they'd go quietly on their way. I had to kill them. It went exactly like you say. I'd only just got the cash when these cattle came burstin' on the scene with a coupla horsemen not far behind. I lit out, sure as shooting. Old Sam Cole would know me by sight. There was a moon that night and I rode a white mare in them days. It's a wonder he kept quiet about it.'

'He couldn't talk without puttin' himself on the spot.'

'I guess not.' The mayor looked fearfully at Abel Davis. 'What are you aimin' to do about all this?' he asked.

'Nothin' at all, Mr Mayor. I was a kid when it happened and you got yourself enough troubles without me addin' to them. I figure as how stories are goin' around town about now. You've already heard the start of them. By the time Ray Bonny's nephews come to town, the word will be out on the street and they won't be takin' too kindly to the fella what got their Uncle Ray killed. Then there's the Hudson family. Lawyer Braddock tells me they're comin' to town as well. They're gonna hear the stories too, and they'll also be on the prod, like as not.'

'You've got to protect me, Abel,' the mayor pleaded. 'You have a future hear while I'm the boss man. I'll get rid of Bert and put you in his place. At double the money. You can do well here. Maybe even get on the council. . . .'

The town was quiet for a week or more but stories were going around. Mayor Ryker got some odd looks as he made an occasional appearance in public. He spent most of the time standing at the window of the funeral parlour, watching the arrival of every horseman and looking thinner and more fretful as the days went by.

When the stage arrived from Tombstone on the Thursday afternoon, he was in his usual position, scanning the passengers in case one of them was a danger to him. He had no reason to worry. The only two who alighted were an elderly lady who was greeted by Mrs Braddock, and a thin young man who did not even carry a gun. He was pale-faced and wearing town clothes. His manner was awkward and he spoke softly to the Wells Fargo agent. The mayor breathed a sigh of relief.

Abel Davis was watching the new arrivals from the window of the jailhouse. He was alone there. The marshal had made himself scarce for the past few days. He knew that if anything happened to the mayor, his career would be over, and he also knew that if anybody tried to kill the First Citizen, it would be better to leave the fighting to his deputy. The marshal had decided to be ill for a week or so.

Abel watched the little old lady being led away

amid a gossiping trio of like-minded women. He eyed the other passenger with some care, wondering if there was a hidden gun somewhere under the dusty coat. The young fellow had only one rather large carpetbag, and after asking directions, he headed off for the Ryker House Hotel. It seemed that he had a bit of money, then, and must be in town on some sort of business.

The deputy returned to his desk and picked up the worn pack of playing-cards. It really felt like his desk now. For all practical purposes, he was marshal of Ryker's Ford. It was a position that did not give him the pleasure it should have done and he sat there shuffling the cards despondently.

It was quite a surprise when the door opened and the man from the stage entered the office. He had got rid of his carpetbag, had washed and brushed up, and looked like some young college fellow from a big Eastern town.

'My name is Walter Parsons, Marshal,' the man said as he held out a pale hand and gave a limp shake. 'I've just got in on the stage and I'm to deal with my uncle's estate. Ray Bonny. You'll have known him, of course.'

'Oh, sure. I knew Ray Bonny,' Abel said as he waved his visitor to a seat. 'I thought you had a brother, Mr Parsons. Lawyer Braddock mentioned there bein' two of you.'

The man smiled. 'Oh, he's too young to travel all this way from Phoenix. Still at school. I just

153

called in to introduce myself. Your office was the first port of call, as you might say, and then I'll pay my respects to the mayor and Mr Stanley. I also have an appointment with a lawyer called Braddock later today.'

'Yeah, I guess you'll be havin' a busy time. Are you takin' over the runnin' of your uncle's businesses here in town?'

The young man shook his head at the idea of running saloons and a brothel.

'Oh, no. I shall sell them off and return home. This looks a prosperous place so it should be possible to get a fair price.'

'I would reckon so,' Abel said slowly. 'Were you close to your uncle, Mr Parsons?'

'Not really. We lads barely knew him, and mother said that he was a rough sort of man.'

Abel managed a smile. 'He was certainly that. Scared the hell outa some folks, he did. Had one gun at his belt and another hid in his coat. Do you carry a gun, Mr Parsons?'

'No, I never felt the need to. I work for a grain-merchant who is one of those Quaker folk. He wouldn't have a gun about the place.'

'I wish more people felt that way. Well, I can only welcome you to Ryker's Ford and wish you the best of luck in your business dealings.'

The two men shook hands again and young Parsons left to go down the street towards the bank.

*

The mayor was on the look-out again the next day. The stage going in the opposite direction was due in at noon and there were several people around the Fargo office waiting to travel to Tombstone or on to Phoenix. Steve Ryker was worried. A young fellow had tried to see him the day before, and been turned away by the mortician's assistant. The mayor knew that the caller was Ray Bonny's nephew and he was frightened to leave the building until the man was out of town. He watched now for any member of the Hudson family stepping off the stage with vengeance in mind.

There were no passengers alighting when the heavy rig eventually pulled into town. The mail was handed down and a strongbox for the bank. People were getting ready to board as soon as the horses were changed and the driver and guard refreshed.

Just as the animals were being harnessed the shot was heard. Everything stopped and people looked around to see from where it had come. They saw Abel Davis dash out of the jailhouse while Len Stanley came to the door of the bank.

It was the Wells Fargo clerk who pointed in the direction of the funeral parlour.

'Over there, Marshal!' he shouted. 'I saw a young fella go in just a minute ago.'

The deputy ran towards the mayor's place of

business just as the door of the building opened. The lawman drew his gun, but it was only Steve Ryker's assistant who stood nervously on the stoop.

'He tried to kill the mayor,' the young man stammered as he moved aside to let the lawman enter.

Young Walter Parsons lay face down on the floor and a Colt .45 was by his right hand. The mayor stood in front of him with another Colt in his fist.

'I had to kill him,' he said flatly. 'He tried to kill me.'

Abel Davis bent down and examined the body. The lad had been shot in the chest at close range. He carried no gun belt and his small pockets could never have housed a large pistol like the Colt.

'He only meant to pay his respects, Mayor,' the lawman said wearily.

'He drew on me!' Steve Ryker shouted. 'Didn't he, Dave?'

The youth nodded dumbly and to the deputy's eyes, seemed to be ashamed of the lie he was telling.

'Yeah, well I guess we have to leave it at that,' the lawman said in a defeated voice. 'You're the mortician, so I reckon it's all your business now.'

He left the building and walked slowly back to the jailhouse. He knew what had happened. The mayor had caught one glimpse of the young man entering the funeral parlour, and had panicked. Steve Ryker was scared rotten and would be for the rest of his life.

Abel watched the stage getting ready to leave. He had lost interest in Ryker's Ford and almost wished he was boarding the rig to some place else. He was just about to turn away from the window and pour a consoling cup of coffee, when another shot echoed round the town.

It took him by surprise but he yanked the door open and ran into the street. The folk round the stage were looking in the direction of the funeral parlour again. The door was still open and Steve Ryker's assistant had been explaining to folks what had happened earlier. The young man had turned round in alarm at the sound of the shot behind him.

Abel Davis reached the door of the little office at the back of the parlour almost as soon as the assistant did. The two of them stood there, gazing at the body that lay face down at the desk.

Steve Ryker had been sitting there when somebody shot him in the centre of the head.

'They must have come in the back door,' the assistant murmured.

Banker Stanley arrived on the scene, panting and sweating as he looked at the dead man.

'You've got a job on your hands now, Marshal,' he wheezed. 'Two of them in one day.'

Abel shook his head. 'Not me,' he replied. 'I've had enough of this town. I got me a hankerin' for roundin' up cattle or horses. Some place well away from folk. Get yourselves a new marshal, Mr

157

Stanley. I quit.'

He pushed past the gathering crowd and went to stand in the fresh air by the Wells Fargo office. The passengers were getting reluctantly aboard the stage. They were missing the excitement but it had to leave promptly. The little old lady who had arrived on Thursday came scurrying round the corner at the last minute. The Wells Fargo man placed her luggage on top and then took her ticket to check the destination.

'To Tombstone and then on to Phoenix and a change to points east,' she told him sweetly. 'Name of Hudson.'

'That's one long journey, ma'am. Pity you ain't got no company with you.'

'It is that, young fella, but I'm an old widow woman and got no kin left these days. All gone before to the Realms of Glory.'

The Wells Fargo agent helped her aboard and closed the door. She nestled a heavy leather hand-bag on her knees and stared out of the window to nod regally to Abel Davis. Her gnarled hands caressed the outline of the gun that the bag concealed. It was still warm after shooting Steve Ryker.